Forget Me Not

WILLOW CREEK BOOK #3

CARRIE JACOBS

to MERF Radio
for providing the soundtrack to my procrastination

"THE FARM"

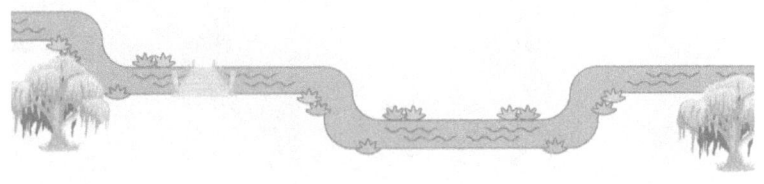

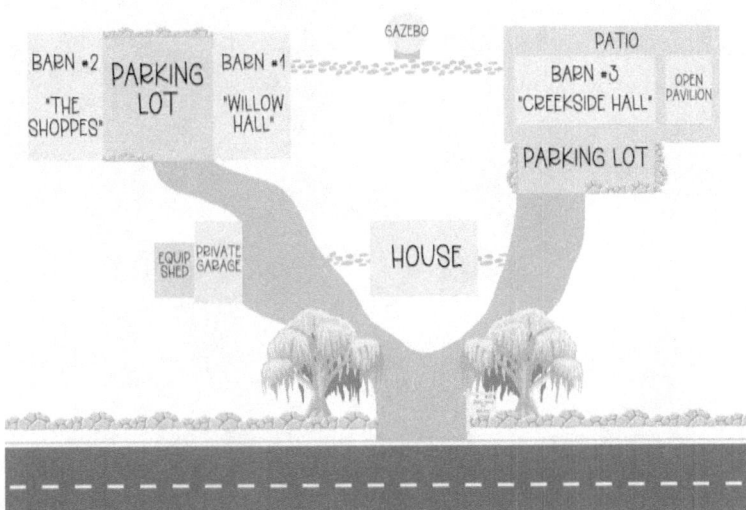

Chapter One

"Whatcha working on?"

Jillian Sullivan gasped and jerked her head up. Instinctively, her hands splayed out to cover up the paper she'd been writing on.

Her brother stood in the doorway to her office, holding a plastic bowl. "Whoa, sorry, I didn't realize you were concentrating so hard." The handle of a fork was visible over the top of the small container.

It was a little disconcerting that she'd been so focused on her task that even the doorbell to her flower shop didn't grab her attention. Especially since there was a buzzer located directly beside the desk in her little office, not even two feet from her head.

She blew out a breath and sat back in her chair. "Gavin. I didn't hear you come in." She frowned. "Did the doorbell go off?"

"I think so?" He shrugged, indicating that he couldn't remember for sure.

Thank goodness it wasn't a customer who'd come in. She

disregarded the thought. Jilly's Blooms was only open by appointment on Saturdays, so a random customer coming in was unlikely. Especially since the entire Willow Creek farm-turned-event-venue was abuzz with activity in preparation for this evening's annual Halloween event. The entire community would be enjoying a whole host of Halloween-themed activities for the whole family, including a haunted hayride, live music from local bands, a costume contest, and, of course, food.

"I brought you some raspberry lava cake that erupted before it was supposed to."

She eagerly accepted the container and inhaled deeply, savoring the fruity chocolate scent. "This smells divine." There were definite perks to having a professional baker in the family.

Gavin dropped into the folding chair facing her desk. "Ready for tonight's festivities?"

She took a bite of the still-warm cake. It was divine. "Absolutely. It's going to be so much fun." Her gaze flicked over to the shimmery ice blue princess ballgown hanging on the door that was perfect for the royal gala theme.

"Summer's really gone all out this year."

Halloween was their sister's favorite holiday to plan events for, and it showed. "I thought she was crazy for buying that twelve-foot-tall skeleton last year, but she's really gotten her money's worth out of it, hasn't she?" Jillian chuckled. The skeleton – named Willow in honor of the farm – proudly stood at the front of the property, holding a giant welcome banner. An entire crew of regular-sized plastic skeletons dotted the rest of the lawn. This year, they were dressed in tuxedos and gowns and positioned as dancers at a ball.

Last Halloween, Summer had dressed them all in denim

and plaid and posed them with stacks of hay bales and farm equipment.

Jillian couldn't begin to imagine what they might be doing next year.

"The weather's perfect. I think we're going to have a massive turnout."

She agreed. "Absolutely. I just heard them talking about it on the radio again, too, so it's really getting some hype. What's your costume?"

"Prince Charming."

Jillian snickered. "I bet Kate got a good laugh about that."

"Hey, now. Leave my wife out of this."

It was hard to believe Gavin and Kate had just celebrated their second anniversary after twenty years apart. It was even harder to believe it had been three and a half years since teenaged Maggie arrived out of the blue and announced that Gavin was her dad. It was the best kind of chaos, adding Maggie, Kate, and Kate's younger son, Lucas, to the family.

Maggie, now twenty-one, went to school and worked part time in Gavin's bakery, Batter Up!, which was right next door to Jillian's flower shop. Literally right next door. Their businesses shared a wall, as they were both housed in a renovated barn named The Shoppes, along with the farm's office, which was upstairs and managed by Summer.

"Working on your fall inventory?"

Jillian's face heated as her hand reached out to cover the page. "No." She pulled in a deep breath and blew it out. She hadn't been planning to tell anyone about the list, but she really wanted to talk about it. "Well… I suppose it's an inventory of sorts." It was more like a list of grievances. Or, more accurately, *former* grievances against her big sister, Summer. She thought of another thing she'd been holding onto for far too long and added it to the list in neat handwriting.

Gavin's brow furrowed in confusion.

"I finally found a therapist my insurance covers, and I really like."

"Took long enough."

"No kidding." After three years of waitlists, insurance preapprovals and rejections, a therapist who openly rolled his eyes, and one who was great but went on maternity leave after their third session, Jillian finally found someone she trusted to help her work through her issues. The biggest one? Her life-long, one-sided feud with Summer. "She gave me homework. It's an exercise we're calling 'Fact or Fiction.' I'm making a list of every single conflict I've ever had with Summer, no matter how small."

He raised a skeptical eyebrow. "It sounds like dwelling on negative stuff from the past. How is that helpful?"

She held up a hand before he could – rightly – remind her (again) that their sister wasn't the villain. "It's helpful because then I go through the list and write down what actually happened, like a journalist. Just the facts, no emotion. It's not about dwelling on things. It's about reframing them and letting them go."

She mostly agreed with her new therapist that the exercise would help her let go of the past, with all its hurts – real and imagined – and build the sort of relationship with her sister that they both deserved, but seeing all her petty gripes listed in black and white made her stomach a bit queasy.

She continued explaining. "Things like Mom and Dad giving her a car. I was upset because I never got a free car so it seemed like favoritism. But then I write down facts about that, like it was Mom's old car that was already paid for. Summer had to drive us to our activities and pay her own insurance and gas, so it wasn't a free car with no strings attached. Stuff like that. It's helping me reframe my memories into what's real and what's distorted. Some I'm just flat-out wrong." She huffed out a sort of laugh as she looked at the sheer amount of line items on the page. "A *lot*, I'm flat-out wrong."

Jillian had only been eleven when Summer was sixteen, so her youth could excuse some of her perception. For instance, she remembered that Summer was always going to the movies with her friends. Without Jillian. What her memory conveniently left out was that Summer *worked* at the movie theater.

In theory, the exercise was simple. In reality, the exercise was draining and made Jillian feel like crap because it did feel like dwelling on negativity and she'd been doing that her whole life. Then again, confronting the negativity was necessary to permanently exorcise it. Her eyes skimmed the list. She'd spent so many years being aggrieved by stupid stuff.

"I'm sure there are a lot of things you're right about, too," Gavin said kindly.

Her gaze flicked to the page and landed on one item. Not specifically about Summer, but the whole family. "At least one."

Gavin leaned forward and put his elbows on her desk.

"The biggest thing isn't just about Summer. It's everybody. Even Nana." That was hard to admit. Nana was always on her side about almost everything.

"Even me?"

"Yeah." Her face heated as she continued. "I feels stupid and petty to say it out loud."

His expression was immediately serious. "Tell me."

"It's ridiculous. I'm going to be forty years old, so this shouldn't bother me."

"Jilly."

Might as well rip off the band aid. She blurted it out. "It's my birthday. I feel like I've never had a birthday where I got to be the center of attention. Everybody's always tired of celebrating and they're busy getting ready to get back to work or driving back home or something. You and Summer always had big pool parties for your birthdays and I had sleepovers that people only came to because their parents wanted to dump them off for free babysitting so they could go to New Year's parties."

Gavin's face scrunched into a sympathetic smile. "I'm sorry I never realized. I guess being a New Year's baby would feel like that, wouldn't it?"

"I know I'm too old for stuff like that to matter." But it did matter, even if she wished it didn't.

"Stop. You're not too old, and it's not silly."

"No, I am, and it is. I'm sure people with Christmas birthdays have it worse."

"So? If you break your leg, it still hurts even though it would be worse to break both legs."

Jillian considered that as she drummed her fingers on the paper. "That's the long and short of it. I put it all on my giant list of petty whining and complaining. Next step is to cross off everything that is unreasonable, address the things that are legit, then burn the evidence in a sort of purging ceremony to let go of everything with the smoke. It's uncomfortable, but I think it'll be a healing exercise for me in the long—"

The walkie talkie on her desk crackled, followed by their mom's hysterical voice shouting, "Jillian! Jillian!"

She snatched the walked and pressed the button. "Copy, what's goi—"

"The flower arch is coming down! At the bridge!"

"Oh, no!" Jillian shoved back from her desk, coming to an abrupt stop as her chair smacked into the filing cabinet. She lunged out of the chair and clipped the walkie to the waistband of her jeans as she raced through the shop, out her door, and through the lobby of The Shoppes. Gavin was close behind as she pushed through the main doors to the parking lot.

Her sneakers smacked the pavement of the parking lot that connected The Shoppes to the original barn, christened Willow Hall after it was remodeled. She sprinted toward the creek, to the wooden bridge that was currently framed by a huge flower arch with spotlights that would show guests where to cross the creek to get in line for a hayride through the neighboring cornfields.

As she approached, she took in the scene. Her parents and brother-in-law wrestled with the top part of the flower arch that had somehow detached from the wooden frame.

"I'm trying not to crush them," Ben said as he held the connected bunch of mums and sunflowers as high over his head as he could.

"It's okay, what happened?" Jillian grabbed the ladder and gave it a quick shake to make sure it was solid before she scrambled up the first few rungs to inspect the wooden arch frame.

Gavin was right behind her. He reached up to relieve some of the strain from Ben.

Her dad explained, "I was going over to check the tractor and saw the top was loose. I called your mom over and by the time she got over from Creekside Hall, it was coming down."

Jillian felt along the joints in the wooden arch. It was sturdy and secure, but shreds of tape stuck to the arch, along with bits of greenery from the flowers. She reached into the flowers and pulled a bit of tape. It fell off easily, like plain paper. "I'm sorry, guys. It's all my fault. I tried a new binding adhesive tape and it's junk." At least the flowers themselves were wired together, so it would only be a matter of reattaching them to the arch.

Footsteps rushed from behind her.

"How can I help? What do you need?" Summer asked from below the arch.

"Zip ties," Jillian answered. "There's a whole box of them on the shelf beside my desk."

Chapter Two

"Ah. I wondered where you'd snuck off to." Theo slipped into their father's opulent home office and quickly closed the door behind him, cutting off the sounds of clinking glasses and fake laughter.

Isaac Frazier chuckled as he looked up at his younger brother. "You're not going to turn me in, are you?" He'd slipped away from his parents' high society version of a Halloween masquerade ball and hid out in the office. Now, he sat at their father's massive desk killing time until guests decided to start leaving so he could make an actual getaway.

Theo snorted. "Psht, not a chance. I had my fill of getting my butt touched by ladies who think their fancy little masquerade masks are enough to conceal their identities. No, Mrs. Baxter, I'd recognize your hyena laugh and grabby mitts anywhere." He loosened his bowtie and flopped onto the deep blue eighteenth-century velvet sofa positioned near the fireplace.

Isaac began, "Money—"

"—doesn't buy class," they finished together.

Isaac had abandoned his own tuxedo jacket, bowtie, and

vest an hour ago when he'd snuck into the office, which was mostly for show. William Frazier III's "real" office was a few miles away in downtown Houston, in the penthouse suite of the Frazier Industries corporate building. Isaac popped open another button on his starched white shirt and leaned back in the plush leather chair.

Isaac much preferred his own office, which was mainly his messenger bag. His physical office was in the Frazier Foundation building next to the one that housed the Frazier Industries offices. Same complex, but the foundation's office building was smaller and much less ostentatious.

The Frazier Foundation was a connected but separate entity from Frazier Industries, even though they were originally one business, started by Isaac's great-great grandmother, Wilhelmina Frazier, in 1930 at the start of the Great Depression.

Theo interrupted Isaac's random line of thought. "I'm not supposed to tell you this."

It wasn't the words, so much as the gravity with which they were delivered, that commanded Isaac's full attention. He raised an eyebrow and waited.

Theo shrugged out of his jacket and tossed it over the arm of the couch, then toed his shiny black shoes off and let them drop to the floor. "Mom's making plans."

"She's always making plans." Isaac relaxed a fraction. The day Victoria Frazier stopped making plans would be the day she stopped drawing breath.

"For you specifically."

Uh oh. "What sort of plans?" Isaac asked warily.

Theo put one hand over his heart and lifted the other to the sky as he quoted Jane Austen. "'It is a truth universally acknowledged, that a single man in possession of a good fortune, must be in want of a wife.' That's what she said to Mrs. Salamander earlier this evening. More or less."

"Salamander?"

"You know. The tall woman with the bird nose." He pinched near the tip of his nose and pulled his fingers outward to demonstrate.

"Salamanca." As he corrected his brother, he recognized the quote from *Pride and Prejudice*. A ball of dread settled into his gut as Theo explained.

"Close enough. Anyway, I wasn't supposed to overhear, but a certain family, including one freshly-divorced Miss Charmaine Delacorte—"

"She's divorced? Again?"

Theo held up fingers as he counted. "Not once, not twice, but thrice. No, wait. Widowed, widowed, so technically this is her first divorce. He was only early sixties and took good care of his health. Guess she didn't want to try waiting this one out."

Isaac laughed at the grim joke, then abruptly stopped. "Hold up. What does she have to do with Mom's plans?"

"She's been added to the guest list for the annual Frazierland trip."

"No." Every year, their parents hosted a big to do at their corporate-owned resort on Frazier Key, a tiny private island in the Gulf of Mexico, just off Tampa. The weeklong event was part business strategy planning, part family events, part schmoozing and greasing important wheels. Theo and Isaac not-so-affectionately dubbed the island Frazierland.

"Yep."

"Whyyyyyy?" Isaac's head dropped back against the leather.

"You know why."

Isaac did know why. His mother had wanted him to end up

with Charmaine since they were teenagers. Not because of any of Charmaine's personal qualities, mind you, but because Charmaine's parents were Aristide and Nicolette Delacorte, who were essentially New Orleans Old Money Royalty. Many years ago, Isaac had gone along with his mother's suggestion to take Charmaine out on a date. To call it a "disaster" would be to grossly minimize the experience.

Theo snickered. "What, you don't want to spend another evening listening to this?" He held his arm up and snapped his fingers six times in rapid succession.

Isaac shuddered, not wanting to remember his mortification as Charmaine snapped her fingers at their server – once directly in his face – and demanded he return her plate to the kitchen because a few of the parsley flakes sprinkled as a garnish on her potatoes had landed upon her peas. The horror.

She also snapped to complain about the temperature of the wine (too cold), the other guests (too loud), and the room (too warm). Then she snapped to call the manager over to complain about a pimple on the server's chin. In short, Charmaine Delacorte was a spoiled brat nightmare and Isaac had zero intention of spending any time with her, even if it irritated his mother. Which it surely would.

Theo broke into his unpleasant trip down Memory Lane. "What ever happened with that woman from Virginia? What's her name? Jill?"

"Jillian. From Pennsylvania."

"Yeah, her."

An image of her smiling face came to mind. "I haven't talked to her in a while." Three months, one week, and six days, to be precise, but who's counting?

"Did she finally shoot you down?"

Isaac shook his head and turned his head to look at his brother. "I never got the nerve to ask her out," he admitted.

Theo sat upright. His eyes squinted and his mouth opened in confusion. "Dude. It's been *years*."

"I know."

"How do you pine for this woman for what, four years? And never get up the nerve to ask her out? Isaac. For real. Why?" For Theo, the gregarious, extroverted life of the party, Isaac's behavior was foreign and unfathomable.

"I don't know. It just never seemed like the right time. Every time I've been to Willow Creek, there's been other stuff going on." Sure, he'd wanted to ask her out a million times, but every time he got close, he choked.

Theo chewed on his bottom lip a moment, frowning, then his eyebrows lifted and his mouth curved into a smile. "Invite her to Frazierland."

The suggestion hit Isaac like a brick to the face. "Are you out of your mind? I haven't even asked her to dinner. How do you expect me to invite her on a weeklong trip to the Island of No Escape?"

"You answered your own question. Every time you see her, there's other stuff going on. This way, you get to spend some time together. I've got it. Beg her to be your buffer person. Maybe she'll take pity on you."

Isaac let the idea roll around in his mind. "It's not the *worst* idea you've ever had. I'd love to get the nerve to invite her, but I don't know if I could. Or should." He trailed off for a minute, then asked, "Are you bringing Gisele so we can finally meet her?"

Theo's eyes darted to the side and his cheeks reddened. He cleared his throat. "She, um, has to work."

He studied his brother's expression. Suspicion took hold and he leaned back in the chair. "You have got to be kidding me."

"What?"

"How did I not see it until now? She doesn't exist. There's no Gisele, is there?"

Theo held his hand up and wiggled it back and forth. "There *is* a Gisele. Or, more accurately, there *was*. There wasn't really a romantic connection so we stopped seeing each other, but it seemed prudent to keep that part to myself."

"I can't even be mad. I just wish I'd thought of it."

"You kind of did. You've been talking about Jillian for a while. I'm sure there are questions about her existence."

"I suppose I could explain that she's in Myanmar with Gisele working for Doctors Without Borders."

Theo snort-laughed. "No, Gisele is in Kyrgyzstan now."

"Right. With no internet or cell service."

"Bingo," Theo said through a massive yawn.

The clock on the wall showed one twenty-six. A.M. Isaac rubbed his eyes. "Why do these things last forever?" Their parents' parties were constant fodder for the high society pages. "I just want to go home and go to bed."

"Same." After a long moment, Theo sat up and patted his hands down the front of his jacket. "Can I see your phone a sec?"

Isaac slid his phone across the shiny desktop. He bit back the urge to scold Theo for losing his phone. Again.

"Okay, let's go." Theo stood and shoved his feet into his shoes.

"Where?" Isaac asked warily.

"Home."

"Yeah, right. You know they have our cars strategically parked in so we can't escape."

"That's why I ordered an Uber."

Isaac shook his head as he tugged his jacket on. "With *my* phone? Your phone isn't lost, is it? You just wanted to use my account."

"Small price to pay for getting you home, isn't it?" Theo smirked and unlocked the tall window that overlooked a large patio that in turn overlooked one of the gardens. "Come on." He slipped out the window and crept across the patio.

Isaac hesitated. Wayward teenagers snuck out their parents' windows in the middle of the night, not men in their early forties. On the other hand, Theo still had his phone. And he really, really wanted to go home. With a sigh, he slung a leg out and climbed into the night. He reached back in to pull the window down. It settled tightly into the sill. No turning back now.

He had to run across the patio and down the stairs to catch up with Theo, who was hunched over, weaving his way through the valet-parked cars.

Theo cast a glance backward over his shoulder. Once Isaac caught up, they silently crept around the cars, avoiding the lights and the security cameras that tripped the alarms, even though they were sure to show up on the regular cameras.

They crouched low at the last car, then fist-bumped and sprinted the ten yards to the main gate like they were dodging armed guards after a diamond heist. They scuttled between the decorative wrought iron posts, leaving the manicured lawn and stone fountain behind them. Once outside, they high fived, then jogged down the block to the closest gas station, laughing the whole way.

"You know Mom's going to have a fit."

Theo shrugged. "If not this, it'd be something else."

"True." Isaac patted his jacket. "Hey. Give my phone back."

Theo handed it over. "There's our ride."

A minute later, they were in the back seat of an SUV, heading toward the apartment building where they both lived when they were in Houston.

Isaac rolled his head from side to side and felt a satisfying crack in his neck. He wasn't a fan of staying up to the wee hours, especially for a party he didn't want to attend in the first place. But being a Frazier meant that schmoozing, at least a little bit, was part of the job.

When they finally rolled up to the apartment building, Isaac was so tired he thought he'd rather just flop onto the sleek sofa in the ultra-modern lobby and avoid the extra minutes it would take to ride the elevator to his floor.

Theo nudged his arm. "You got your keycard?"

"Sure," he mumbled and pulled his card out of his wallet. He tapped it on the little black box that unlocked the main door.

They rode up the elevator in tired silence and got off on the seventh floor. Theo turned to go right, while Isaac turned left.

As they parted, Theo said, "Let me know what she says."

"What? Who?"

Theo just snickered and turned the corner, and Isaac was too tired to figure out what his brother was talking about.

Chapter Three

It was well after midnight when the tractor finally delivered the last of the hayride guests back to the bridge after the final run of the night. Its steady rumbling had been background noise for hours, and now, after the remaining cars pulled away, silence settled over the farm.

Jillian shivered as she helped with her part of grabbing any obvious trash and tossing it in the dumpster. The rest of the staff had already torn down canopies and taken stray tables and chairs inside the buildings to be dealt with in the morning.

She slipped into The Shoppes. Batter Up! was dark, so she assumed Gavin and Kate had already left.

Being alone in the shop late at night was always a little eerie. Leaves and greenery had sharp edges that created sinister-looking shadows and deep layers of darkness in the corners.

It didn't help that she'd spent all night surrounded by ghouls and goblins and the excited screams of people enjoying the haunted activities.

The thin tulle sleeves of her princess gown had done nothing to keep her arms warm as the night got progressively chillier. She debated changing back into her regular clothes, but decided against it. No sense changing now and changing into her pajamas when she got home in fifteen minutes, so she grabbed her tote bag and hooked it over her shoulder.

She looked inside and realized the list wasn't in her bag. With a start, she remembered leaving it on her desk when she ran out to fix the arch. On her desk. Where the box of zip ties had been placed.

Her stomach clenched. If Summer had put the zip ties back... oh, no. The list was right there. Summer had to have seen it when she got the zip ties in the first place. Jillian's heart stuttered a little as she took a step toward her desk.

There was a tiny possibility she hadn't seen the list, right? When they were fixing the arch she might have been in a hurry and not seen it, right? Jillian tried to remember how long Summer had been gone after she'd inside for the zip ties, but she couldn't calculate any sort of answer.

She blew out a long breath. What the heck could she do now?

The tote bag thunked as she dropped it to the floor. All she could do now was cross her fingers and hope Summer hadn't seen the list. If she had, she surely would have said something. Or acted different. Right?

Then again, had they even interacted throughout the event? Jillian couldn't remember. She'd been so busy handing out candy and small toys and taking photos that she couldn't recall seeing her sister all evening.

Okay. She'd hide the list, stay away from the farm all day Sunday, and then when Monday came, she'd play it by ear. Or interrogate Gavin. If Summer found the list, she'd surely go to him first.

She rounded the desk and grabbed the box of zip ties. She set it on the shelf where they belonged, then reached for the list. Only… there was no list. The only thing under the box was her desk calendar, a large rectangle full of scribbled appointments and notes for ordering which flowers for what event.

No list.

Her knees turned to jelly. Blue tulle fluttered outward as she sank down onto her chair.

First, she lifted the calendar. Nothing underneath. She flipped every page. Nothing. She pulled open her desk drawers, one by one. Nothing.

Her insides went ice cold in a way that had nothing to do with the temperature. She crossed her arms, hugging herself, but there was no comfort in her numb, tingling fingers.

"What do I do? What do I do?" she whispered to the empty room. Normally, she'd run straight to Nana, who would assure her she was fine, and then give her advice. But Nana had gone to Ohio for a whole month to visit her sister and some cousins, so Jillian was on her own.

She did the only thing she could think of. She grabbed her tote bag and purse and locked up as fast as she could, then scurried out of The Shoppes, hoping against hope that she wouldn't be seen.

The tiniest wave of relief hit her in the parking lot when her car was the only one remaining, which meant Summer had already left. She released a white cloud of breath into the night. It drifted skyward into the darkness above the light illuminating the parking lot.

A stray candy wrapper caught her attention, but it was late, she was exhausted, and she felt exposed standing out in the open, so she ignored it and jumped into her car.

In her driveway a few minutes later, she rifled through her tote bag again. She didn't think the list was in there, but it was possible, wasn't it? Maybe?

No.

She distinctly remembered looking at the list with Gavin, and then the walkie had gone off and she'd run without touching the list again. Gavin had been right behind her.

Which only left one option. Summer saw it when she got the zip ties.

Jillian leaned forward and rested her forehead on the steering wheel. Summer had the list. Summer was going to see every petty grievance and have no context. She was going to think those things were how Jillian really felt, which couldn't be farther from the truth. Yes, she *had* felt a certain way, but she'd grown and evolved past those feelings and could recognize them for the insignificant – and wrong – items they truly were.

Tears stung the backs of her eyes. Whatever Summer did to her, she deserved.

She should never have done the exercise.

No, that wasn't it. She could definitely see the value in purging all the negativity and ceremonially destroying it.

She should never have done the exercise in the shop, where there was always a chance of it being discovered.

Yep, that was the answer. She'd been careless. For Pete's sake, they all worked in the same building. What was she thinking?

The tears let loose. Tears full of frustration at herself for her foolishness – not only for leaving the list somewhere it could easily be found, but for having it there at all. She should have made the list on her phone or done the exercise at home. She reached out without looking and rooted in her tote bag for a tissue.

She blew her nose and turned the car off. Immediately, she felt the absence of heat, so she grabbed her bag and hurried for the front door to let herself inside. The house was warm, at least. She rubbed her arms and headed straight for the bedroom. Even though it was late, she decided to take a hot shower. Maybe it would warm her up and wash away some of the negative feelings that were overwhelming her.

But probably not.

She couldn't blame any of this on anyone but herself.

Which meant no one but her could fix it.

She stood under the hot water, letting it rain down over her head and warm her all the way to her toes. When she was done, she felt cleaner, but not any better. She dressed in her warm pajamas and fuzzy socks and climbed into bed.

Sleep eluded her. At four, she decided to try scrolling through some social media. Maybe that would help.

She fished in her purse for her phone and entered the unlock code.

Her finger hovered above the screen. There was a notification for a text message.

From Isaac.

Her heart skipped a beat. She hadn't heard anything from him for a few months, so she assumed he'd moved on from Willow Creek for good. She pulled a deep breath and opened his message. It was a huge block of text.

> Hey Jillian, I've missed talking to you! This is going to be out of left field, but I'm in a bind. Would you be interested/able to go to Florida with me for a few days this coming week? It's a sort of Frazier business/family thing and I could really use a friend as a buffer lol. I'm know it's super short notice and a crazy ask, but I'd really like to see you. It's at a resort, so lots to do. Again, I'm so sorry for the short notice but it took me forever to get up the nerve to even ask. If not, no problem, I promise!

Jillian stared at the message. It had come in at two o'clock. Was he drunk or something? She mentally ran over the things she needed to do for the upcoming week. There wasn't much in the way of client-facing items. Just lots of back-end tasks like inventory and updating her website and sending a newsletter.

Wait. She snuggled deeper under the thick comforter. Was she really considering this? Why? Just to escape?

Maybe.

Escaping probably wasn't the worst idea. It would give Summer a few days to get over the biggest part of the anger she was surely feeling. There was a wedding coming up the first weekend in December that would pull the bulk of Summer's attention after the next week, so maybe it wasn't just not a bad idea, maybe it was a *good* idea. Take a little space. A lot of space. Pennsylvania to Florida seemed like just the right amount of space.

She'd get to see Isaac.

And put off facing the music for a few days so she could get her mental ducks in a row and build up the strength she'd need to face Summer's completely justified anger and hurt.

Before she could change her mind, she typed a reply.

> Yes! Perfect timing, let me know the details.

She hesitated, then pressed the button to send the message.

Chapter Four

Isaac slept in on Sunday morning. It was almost nine when he finally stretched and debated whether to get up or roll over and catch a few more minutes of sleep.

His phone vibrated once, twice, then three times with incoming texts, thwarting his plan to stay in bed. Half a second later, it vibrated with an incoming call. He groaned and rolled toward the night stand to grab his phone.

The texts were from Theo. The call was from his mom.

He let the call go to voicemail and swiped into his messaging app. In addition to Theo's texts, there was one from Jillian.

He grinned up at the ceiling. He'd been trying to gather the nerve to call her or message her or reach out somehow, but he hadn't been able to find either the nerve or a suitable excuse to do so.

Both of Theo's messages were warnings that their mother would be calling.

"Too little, too late, Theo," Isaac mumbled. He backed out of the text thread with his brother and tapped into Jillian's message.

Yes! Perfect timing, let me know the details.

He frowned. What was she talking about? It took a second to focus on the block of text above her message.

A block of text that had gone from him to her.

Hold up. What?

He skimmed over the message and sat bolt upright. He never sent her a message. How could this possibly—

Theo.

He didn't know if he wanted to thank him or strangle him. Maybe a bit of both.

He suddenly wondered why he was thinking about Theo at all, when he should be thinking about Jillian.

Jillian.

Said yes.

To spending a week in Frazierland.

With him.

What??

She had to have misunderstood.

Isaac flopped back onto his pillows and reached down to whip the comforter off, but just stared up at the ceiling instead of moving. Now what?

His phone vibrated again. He sighed and swiped to answer it. "Hey, Mom."

"Don't you 'Hey, Mom' me. What were you thinking, sneaking out with your brother like that in the middle of my party?"

"It was late. We wanted to get home. It's not that deep." He was in no mood for a guilt trip. He'd shown up and stayed until the middle of the night, and that still wasn't good enough.

"It was humiliating. I had to answer questions all night about where you were."

He rolled his eyes. "Oh, stop. We didn't even leave until after one thirty, and I'm sure nobody cared."

"I cared. That should count for something."

Isaac wasn't falling for that tired old guilt trip.

"Charmaine was especially disappointed you weren't there for the last dance."

The mention of her name irritated him. This matchmaking delusion of his mother's needed to stop. "You can drop that right now."

"Drop what?"

"The whole Charmaine thing you're concocting in your head. It's not happening. Ever."

There was a long pause. Then she said, "Isaac. I don't know what you mean."

"I'm hanging up."

"All right, all right. I know you and Charmaine didn't hit it off properly, but that's been several years. She's changed quite a bit."

"No." He doubted a full lobotomy could change her enough to make her tolerable.

"Isaac. You'd make a stunning couple. Think how beautiful your children would be."

Children? With her? Eww. "No."

"One date."

"No."

Another long pause, and then, "Maybe next week will change your mind." She'd delivered the words with that irritating sing-song voice she used when she was sure she knew something you didn't know.

But Isaac did know. Thanks, Theo. "I'm bringing Jillian to Frazierland, so no, I won't be entertaining Charmaine."

His mother smoothly answered, "Sorry, she can't come.

This doesn't give me enough notice to prepare for another person."

"Then you can prepare for one less," he fired back immediately."

"The business portion is mandatory. You can't just back out."

"I can, actually."

There was another lengthy pause and he could feel the wheels turning in his mother's brain, trying to determine how serious he was.

"Isaac." Her tone was suddenly sharp. "Don't make me—"

He cut her off. "Don't start making threats and acting like you're going to fire me, because one of these days I'll call your bluff." It was a common manipulation tactic she used, even though it never really worked on him or Theo. It did, however, seem to work on Four (the nickname for the oldest brother, William IV) and Anthony Frazier-Sheffield, his brother-in-law who was married to his sister, Caroline (he added the Frazier to his name). Sometimes his mom forgot which strategy she needed to use when she started trying to get her way.

"I don't understand why you didn't tell me before now that this person is coming."

"I guess it slipped my mind. Anyway, I have a bunch of details to attend to, soooo…"

She made a small, unconvinced noise. "Mm. Well, remove your car from the lawn."

"I'll get it as soon as I can."

She disconnected the call and he almost breathed a sigh of relief, until he realized he needed to call Jillian and get the situation sorted out. He really, really hoped she was serious about joining him, because explaining yet another change of plans to his mother would be seen as nothing short of anarchy.

He stared at his phone, trying to summon the courage to

call Jillian. It didn't come, so he got up and brushed his teeth and got dressed in his typical casual Sunday uniform of beige pants and a nondescript polo shirt. Since he'd gotten that far, he figured he might as well eat some breakfast. And do a load of laundry.

His apartment had a small stacked washer and dryer in the master bathroom. Standard issue for the apartments in this building that was owned by Frazier industries. Isaac was grateful for the landing pad, identical to Theo's, on the opposite side of the building. Their apartments were just two in a building full of part-time lived-in apartments for the higher ups of both Frazier Industries and The Frazier Foundation. It had lots of amenities like a gym, a pool, and an on-site coffee shop, but it definitely wasn't home. That would be his cozy townhouse in New York. Sort of. It wasn't really home, either, but at least it was all his.

Once the washing machine was set, he started the coffee maker. Eventually, he sat at the table, his mug and his phone in front of him.

He read the message Theo had sent Jillian, then read it again. Theo, who was allergic to punctuation and proper sentence structure when texting, had managed to craft a message that was pretty close to what Isaac would have sent. If he had sent a message. Which he never would have, no matter how much he wanted to. And he did want to. Had wanted to since the day he first saw Jillian Sullivan with her tray of flowers. He remembered everything about that moment. Her long blonde hair was tied back in a low ponytail, with stray bits of hair framing her face. Her bright blue eyes held amusement as he spilled his papers and stumbled over his words.

For some reason, his brothers had inherited all the swagger and charm and effortless flirting, leaving Isaac with a shyness that was inexplicable to the rest of the Frazier clan. He didn't understand it. He was a whiz at easily conversing with clients and new people, but romantically he was hopeless.

He was also a hopeless romantic and believed his One True Love was out there. He'd also suspected that it might be Jillian, from the first time he saw her, but he was too much of a chicken to even ask her out.

Yes! Perfect timing, let me know the details.

He read and reread her message. The reread his/Theo's message again. Was there any way she could have misunderstood? Nope. It was crystal clear that she was being invited. Theo had covered the date, place, and situation succinctly. And she said yes.

Isaac steeled himself. The hard part was over, right? Now it was just a matter of ironing out specific details. Which meant he had to call her.

His fingers trembled a little, but he tapped the phone and before he could change his mind, it was ringing, and before he could hang up and barf, Jillian answered.

"Hi!"

"Jillian," he said in a breath. He cleared his throat. "Jillian. Hey. Hi. How are you?"

"Good. Great. Fine. How are you?" She sounded happy to hear from him.

"Yeah. Uh, I mean, good. Good. Good." He rapped a fist against his chest to make himself shut up.

"Good."

He sat straighter and tried to approach this like a business meeting. "I wanted to touch base and iron out the details and all that. This is, um, a weird business family combo thing we do every year. It's mostly the family and a few higher ups and their families. It's Monday through Friday. Tuesday and

Wednesday are strategic planning meetings for the next year, but it's pretty high level stuff, so only a few hours each day. There's a spa and lots of stuff to do if you want, and of course it's all inclusive, so there won't be any expenses. Except maybe getting to the airport. Of course your flight is covered, and that's part of why I called. To get the info so we can book your flight..." He trailed off, realizing he was rambling.

"Yeah, okay. It sounds good."

He relaxed a fraction. It was definitely easier to treat this like a business consultation. "I'm in Houston right now, so I'll be meeting you in Tampa, if that's okay. If you don't mind flying down alone."

"Yeah. That's not a problem."

"Great! I'll have my assistant call you in a few minutes so she can get the flight information to you directly instead of me trying to be a middle man and messing something up."

"Okay."

"Her name's Alexis. Let me text you her number so you'll recognize it when it comes up."

"Okay."

He copied Alexis's number and texted it to Jillian. "Awesome. So then I'll see you tomorrow in Tampa."

"Great."

"Great. I'm really looking forward to it." He felt like he should say something, anything, to keep the conversation going, but this was painfully awkward.

"Me, too."

"Wonderful. Let Alexis know if you need anything. Or me, of course. You can let me know if you need anything."

"Okay."

"Perfect. See you tomorrow. Bye!"

"Bye."

Isaac disconnected the call and immediately leaned

forward and bonked his head onto the table once, twice, three times. "I'm such an idiot," he muttered. He put his shoes on and grabbed his keys.

The hallway was empty as he walked to Theo's door and knocked.

When Theo opened the door, Isaac held up his phone with the text messages on the screen. "You've got some explaining to do."

Theo snatched his phone and grinned at the screen. "She's going? That's great! You're welcome." He tapped on Isaac's phone.

"What are you doing?"

Theo smirked and handed his phone back. "Ordering an Uber so we can go get our cars."

"Again? Theo. Quit spending my money."

"I'll cash app you."

"When?"

Theo snickered as he put his foot on the arm of the couch to tie his running shoes. "Probably never. But Jillian's coming to Frazierland thanks to me, so I'd call it even."

"Even? You probably owe me ten thousand dollars," Isaac grumbled.

"Not a chance."

They rode the elevator down to the lobby with Theo grinning the whole way. Isaac still wasn't sure if he wanted to thank him or throttle him.

Chapter Five

Jillian stared at the phone in her hand. What was even happening? While she was contemplating Isaac's odd tone, the phone rang with an incoming call from his assistant's number. What was her name again?

"Hello?"

"Hi, Ms. Sullivan, this is Alexis. Mr. Frazier asked me to reach out to you and schedule a flight for tomorrow." She sounded warm and friendly.

"Uh, yeah. Yes." She heard the sound of typing in the background.

"Mr. Frazier said you'll be flying out of Harrisburg?"

Was she really going through with this? "Yes, please."

"Certainly." She paused and typed some more. "Unfortunately, there aren't any direct flights to Tampa. I have one with a brief layover in Atlanta, and one with a brief layover in Charlotte, which does leave a little later in the morning. Do you have a preference?"

"No, either one is fine with me."

"Okay, let me get some information from you."

Jillian answered her questions and a few minutes later,

Alexis said, "I'm very sorry, first class is booked full, so I'm only able to get you a seat in business class."

"Um, that's fine?" She'd never flown anything other than regular mass peon class.

"Will you need more than one checked bag?"

"No?"

More typing, then Alexis cheerfully said, "Okay, you're all booked. You'll leave Harrisburg at eight thirty-five, layover in Charlotte, and then you'll get to Tampa at one o'clock. I've emailed you the confirmation. Would you like me to hold while you check that you've received it?"

"Um, sure." Jillian pulled her phone away from her ear and tapped into her email app. The confirmation from Alexis was in her inbox. "Yes, I've received it."

"Perfect. I'm also emailing you an itinerary for the week, which includes suggestions for what to pack. There's only one formal event. Otherwise, casual is fine."

"Formal?" What was she getting herself into?

"Between you and me, it's not *super* formal. Whatever black cocktail dress you already have will be perfect."

"Oh." Jillian wracked her brain. Did she even own a black cocktail dress? Probably not. And she only had – she glanced at the clock – six hours to find one. "Okay."

There was a long pause, then Alexis said, "Since this is your first visit to Frazier Key, might it be helpful if I included some photos of the typical attire our guests wear?"

Jillian swallowed hard. "I believe that could be helpful, thank you."

"Perfect."

She'd never felt more like a backwoods hick than she did at this very moment.

"Don't hesitate to reach out if you need anything else. You can call or text this number any time."

"Great. Thank you so much."

"You're quite welcome." Alexis ended the call.

Jillian slowly sat down at the kitchen table. What was she thinking by going along with this? Formalwear? Business class flight? Just to avoid Summer?

Summer. The thought sobered her. Yup, creating some space was the best thing she could possibly do right now.

She scrolled through Alexis's new email. The casual clothes were definitely not what she would have thought of as casual. *Business* casual, maybe. Lots of khaki and high-end linen. She sighed. Her closet was full of denim and low-end cotton. Maybe she'd be able to hole up in her room and be invisible.

At least she would definitely not need any more than one checked bag.

She wheeled her ancient, battered suitcase out of the back of her closet and tried to put together some outfits. When that failed, she made a trip to Kohl's, but everything on display was cold-weather clothing. She made three more stops before she got too frustrated to continue. In the Target parking lot, she called Kate, Gavin's wife.

"Hey, Jillian, what's up?"

"I'm desperate."

"Oh, no. Is everything okay?"

She had no idea how to answer that. "Um, it's complicated. I can't give details because it's all just crazy, but do you have a black cocktail dress I can borrow?"

"Are you kidding? I have a whole closet full of them. Come over and take your pick."

Jillian nearly wilted with relief. She knew that Kate, a superstar chef, had worked a lot of formal events for her uber-rich private clients, so she'd hoped she might have something suitable. "Thank you so much. I'll be over." Before she hung up, she asked, "Is Gavin home?"

"No, he took Lucas to the gym for some basketball practice."

"Perfect. I'll be there in twenty minutes."

She drove to Kate and Gavin's house and knocked on the door.

Kate opened the door with an eyeroll. "You can just come in, you know."

"I know, I know."

"I pulled a few things out." Kate led Jillian up the stairs to the master bedroom. Several black dresses hung on the back of the closet door. "I wasn't sure how formal you meant, so here are a couple of tea-length and a full-length."

"I have no idea." She debated how much to tell Kate. "If I tell you something, can you not tell Gavin? I promise I'll tell him myself, but not right now."

Kate hesitated. "As long as it's nothing I feel like he needs to know. You know our history with keeping secrets."

Jillian did know. Kate had given birth to Gavin's child and never told him until Maggie herself sought Gavin out when she was eighteen. "I promise, it's just about me. Nothing bad." She reached out and ran a hand down the lace of the closest cocktail dress. "Isaac invited me to spend the week on his family's island. It's some hybrid business-family annual meeting reunion sort of thing."

Kate's jaw dropped. "No kidding! I had no idea you guys were getting anywhere near that level of serious."

"We're not? I mean, it was out of the blue and last minute. I haven't even talked to him for ages, and to be honest, I thought it might be a scam until I talked to him. I'm leaving in the morning and I'll be back Friday. But I don't know what to wear at all. Isaac's assistant was super helpful and sent me some wardrobe ideas." She opened the email on her phone and showed Kate the pictures Alexis had sent.

"Do you have anything like this?" Kate frowned.

"Not really."

"I got you. Try on the dresses and see what you like. I'll be right back."

Jillian tried on the first dress. It fit, but the v-neck was a bit deeper than she preferred. She was in the second dress, turning from side to side to look in the mirror when Kate came back, wrestling with a large plastic tote. She put it on the floor with a loud thump. "Oooh, that looks amazing on you."

"Do you think so?" The fabric had the slightest blue sheen in the black. It was a simple cut that was similar to the sundresses Jillian wore in the summer.

"Definitely." She popped the lid off the tote. "It's going to be warm during the day, so here's my summer stuff that's more businessy. Go through and take whatever you want."

Jillian sorted through the clothes. They were exactly in the vein that Alexis had sent her. Longer khaki shorts and capris, sleeveless button shirts, and lightweight cardigans. "I promise I'll take care of everything and bring it all back in perfect condition."

Kate said with a laugh, "Don't say that. You'll invite a tsunami of red wine into the whole suitcase."

The thought horrified Jillian. If that happened – probably not wine, but any other disaster could easily befall the clothes – she had no idea how she'd be able to repay Kate. Almost all the clothes had designer labels. Maybe she shouldn't borrow them.

As if Kate read her mind, she said, "I bought most of this stuff secondhand when I was in Orlando and needed more upscale clothes to mingle with my clients. Even if there *is* a red wine tsunami, it's no big deal, I promise. I don't think I've worn any of this for a few years."

"Are you sure?"

"If I wasn't sure, I wouldn't have lugged the tote out of the attic." She shook her head a little. "I really like this dress on you. Take it, and try that one, too."

Jillian took the dress off and tried on the one Kate had suggested. She shifted back and forth so the dress swished around her knees. "I really like this one, too. Now I'm not sure what to do."

"Take them both, obviously. You can pick when you have a better feel for the vibe." Kate stacked the chosen clothes onto a pile. "Do you have a suitcase?"

"Yeah. It's kind of crappy, but it does the job."

Kate eyed her. "Is it something you don't mind Isaac's family seeing?"

"Ugh." She hadn't considered the possibility that anyone would be seeing it, but Kate was right. A partially duct-taped suitcase would probably not portray the right image, even if it was still functional.

"I got you." Kate disappeared for a minute and came back from the attic with a sapphire blue suitcase that looked brand new.

"Kate. I can't—"

"Oh, hush. It's a suitcase." She ignored Jillian's protestations and put the open suitcase on her cedar chest and loaded the clothes into it. "I'll lend you anything you want, but you're on your own to fold it," she said with a laugh.

"You're amazing."

"I am." She chuckled and slung an arm around Jillian's shoulders. "Keep me on speed dial. I expect status updates every six hours."

Jillian laughed with her sister-in-law. "I'll see what I can do."

By six thirty Monday morning, Jillian was through security. She sat at her gate in Harrisburg, holding an iced coffee from Dunkin' that she'd gotten on her way through the airport but hadn't taken a single sip of.

What the heck was she doing? Why was she running away? Oh, right. Because that's what she always did. Stew in silence, keep everything inside, and when things get uncomfortable, bolt or lash out. She couldn't lash out, because this was completely, totally, one hundred percent on herself, so bolting was the more palatable option.

Even though it was jumping from the frying pan into the fire as far as being uncomfortable went, the idea of letting Summer confront her was more than she could bear at the moment. Meeting Isaac's family would also be painful, but at least that level of painful wouldn't come with a mountain-sized helping of guilt on the side.

Slowly, the other seats gained occupants until there were a few dozen people waiting.

Jillian looked at the boarding pass on her app for the thousandth time, but even so she was startled to be in one of the first groups called to board. She scanned her boarding pass and hurried down the hallway with the gaudy hotel carpeting to her plane. The flight attendant greeted her with a big smile. Jillian smiled in return and easily found her seat. She stowed her carryon bag in the overhead compartment and settled into her window seat.

Immediately she was conscious of how different the seats were in business class. Not only did she have several inches to spare on the seat, she had legroom. Legroom! Such amenities were unheard of on the level of flights she could afford herself.

She held her iced coffee and took a series of deep breaths that were supposed to be calming but didn't really do much to help her racing mind.

Was this ridiculous? What was Isaac expecting from this? She startled as she realized how little she'd thought about Isaac and seeing him. She'd been so focused on escaping Summer's justified wrath. She turned to the window and let out a long sigh. Now she felt even guiltier.

Maybe she should get up and get off the plane. Nip this in the bud, go home and face the consequences of her actions. Sit down and have a grown up conversation with her sister, face to face, and explain everything. Finding the list couldn't have been pleasant, but Summer obviously knew they had a tense relationship, so it probably wasn't a terrible shock. Summer was reasonable. Once she got past the initial hurt and anger, she'd understand. Surely.

She reached for the silver buckle resting at her midsection. She wanted to make changes before she turned forty, so now was the perfect opportunity to stop running and start facing things. Handle things differently. It was time to woman up and deal with things head on. Starting now.

She popped the seatbelt open. Her legs tensed to stand.

The flight attendant slammed the door shut and secured it.

Jillian wilted back against her seat.

Figures. For once in her life she gets a wave of courage and is immediately thwarted.

She refastened her seatbelt and sat back, stuck in her own loop of unhelpful thoughts until they landed in Charlotte. Then she was too busy running to her next gate to think.

Before she knew it, it was one o'clock and she was in Tampa.

She grabbed her carryon bag and headed from the frying pan into the fire.

Chapter Six

Isaac sat on the edge of the hard molded chair at baggage claim in Tampa, waiting for suitcases to start spitting out onto the silver carousel across the room. Jillian's plane had arrived on time, judging from the arrivals board he'd checked at least a dozen times.

His own suitcase had taken a ride on the carousel when his flight arrived two hours earlier. Since then, he'd passed the time by scrolling on his phone and people watching.

Passengers from Jillian's flight started arriving, milling around the carousel, waiting for the bags to come through the plastic curtain covering the hole in the wall.

This was it. In a matter of minutes, maybe seconds, he'd see her. His mouth went dry as more people came to baggage claim, but Jillian wasn't part of the crowd. He stood and smoothed the front of his shirt down. It looked like most of the passengers had gathered, but still no Jillian.

Had she missed the connection in Charlotte? Had she decided not to come? He drummed his fingers on the handle of his suitcase.

The telltale clunk and swooshing noise of the conveyor

coming to life had the crowd close in around the carousel, but Jillian still hadn't arrived.

Isaac scanned the area, turning to check the escalators behind him, but there was no one. He swallowed hard. This was not getting off to a great start.

Then he turned back and there she was, hustling from the main area with her carryon bag in one hand and a fast food cup in the other. His heart leapt. She came. She was here. To see him. He could hardly believe it was really happening.

Suitcases slid out from under the plastic curtain and people lunged forward to check the tags and grab their luggage.

Isaac stayed off to the side, watching. Jillian's long blonde hair was pulled up in a messy bun. She wore a white t-shirt with a navy blue cardigan and jeans. Black Converse completed the casual outfit.

The crowd slowly thinned as people grabbed their bags and disappeared toward the exits. She still hadn't noticed him.

He watched her watching the bags until she jumped to attention and leaned forward to grab a blue suitcase from the conveyor belt. She moved backwards, settling her carryon bag on top of the suitcase and then she finally looked around.

The second her eyes found him, a flood of warmth ran through him. She smiled and came toward him. His feet rooted to the floor. He wasn't sure he'd be able to move without falling over if he tried to take a step. It was like watching the sun rise over the horizon after a week of cold, dreary rain.

"Isaac."

"Jillian." He had no idea what to do next. Should he hug her? Shake her hand? Pat her shoulder? Okay, definitely not that.

She shook her cup, making the ice bounce around loudly inside. "I didn't realize you were here waiting. I had to stop and grab something quick to eat. I was starving. I thought I'd have time to get something in Charlotte, but I had to run to catch my connection. Have you been here long?"

It took a beat to register that she'd asked him a question because he was so busy watching her face as she talked. "Yeah. A while. Not because of you," he quickly explained. "My flight got in like two hours ago so I've just been hanging out."

"Oh, my. How long was your flight from Houston?"

"It's pretty short, just a little over two hours." He gestured toward the doors at the far end of the building. "The car is here. Did you need anything else?"

"Nope."

"Can I get your bag for you?" He reached out, but snatched his hand back as she shook her head.

"I've got it, thanks."

He grabbed the handle of his own suitcase and rolled it as she fell in step beside him. They passed a cobalt blue bank of elevators and followed the sign to the sliding doors that led to the outside.

"Wow, it's hot," she said as the wall of heat hit them both.

"Really?" He felt silly for saying it. Obviously she'd come from Pennsylvania, where it's chilly heading into cold this time of year, and not Houston, where it was just as warm.

"It's nice. Believe me, I'm not complaining."

"I didn't think you were."

"Mr. Frazier?" A man in a dark suit grabbed his attention.

Isaac looked up. "Oh! David. Sorry, I thought you were parked over there."

David opened the hatch on the sleek black SUV.

Jillian unhooked the strap of her carryon from the suitcase handle and made a move to put it in the back of the vehicle.

"I'll get that for you, ma'am," David said as he smoothly took the bag from her with one hand and picked up her suitcase with the other. He carefully stowed the bags, then loaded Isaac's suitcase.

After the hatch was secured, David opened the back door for Jillian while Isaac rounded the SUV and got in beside her.

A few minutes later, the airport was behind them. Isaac felt the nerves flutter in his throat. He couldn't think of a single thing to say to her.

"How far is it to the resort?" Jillian asked.

He latched onto the topic. "Not terribly far. We're only twenty minutes away from the helipad, then it's just a twenty minute ride to the island. We'll be there in under an hour, traffic permitting."

"From the what?!" She jerked upright in her seat. "Did you say helipad? As in helicopters? Isaac?"

He wasn't sure what to make of her shock. "I'm sorry. I thought Alexis gave you an itinerary."

"For the resort and for the flight. There was no mention of a helicopter. Are we seriously getting in a helicopter?"

"Yes?" He wracked his brain for other ways to get to the island. "We could charter a boat if that would make you more comfortable." He pulled his phone out. "I'll have Alexis organize it right away."

She leaned back against the seat, tense and stiff. "No, no, don't make a fuss. I've just never been on a helicopter. It seems scary."

Isaac shifted toward her. "It's not much different than being in a plane. Louder, but you'll have a headset, and it's quick. Only twenty minutes. But if you're not up for it, it's truly no problem to have a boat take us out." He lifted his phone. "It's no trouble at all, and I bet it wouldn't even set us back more than a few minutes. I'm really sorry. The helicopter didn't even occur to me."

"It's fine. It's only twenty minutes, how bad can it be, right?"

"If you don't mind flying, it's not bad at all, I promise."

As he spoke, they pulled into the heliport. David parked the SUV and opened Jillian's door before retrieving the luggage and spiriting it away to the helicopter.

Isaac could feel Jillian's hesitation and for the millionth time he thought this might have been a terrible idea. They went from casual flirting – if you could even call it that – a few times a year to all of a sudden being on vacation together. Well, a *sort* of vacation, where they'd be spending an awful lot of time together. With his family. Odds were good that it would scare her off and he'd lose her forever before he ever really had her.

They walked over to the helicopter, a large, sleek, state-of-the-art machine with tons of glass, and metallic green paint that made him think of a dragonfly. A trio of long gray blades topped the roof. They seemed too skinny to support the machine, but he wouldn't be saying that out loud.

Isaac reached out to shake the pilot's hand. "Marvin, how are you?"

"Isaac. Good to see you."

"This is Jillian. It's her first helicopter ride." Before he could say anything else, Marvin's face broke into a warm grin.

"How wonderful! Let me give you a tour and tell you what to expect."

Isaac waited while Marvin excitedly took Jillian all the way around the helicopter, pointing out the parts and compartments and bells and whistles. Then he showed her the cockpit and gave her a brief overview of the complicated instrument cluster all while describing the noises she'd be hearing and what they probably were.

"Since we're flying over the water, the fanny pack is

required," Marvin explained with a wink as he helped fit Jillian's life preserver to her midsection. Then he helped her up into her seat and showed her how to operate the door.

By the time the door closed, she looked calm and ready to go.

Once all three of them were buckled into their seats, Marvin asked, "Are you prone to motion sickness?"

Isaac saw Jillan's eyes widen. "No? Not usually?"

"Excellent. Then we can do a few loopdeloops."

"What?!" Her fingers dug into the sides of her seat.

Marvin laughed. "Kidding, kidding. We've got some great weather, low air speeds today, so it should be a very steady flight." He instructed them to put their headsets on, then flipped some switches and tapped some buttons on the electronic dashboard.

Overhead, the blades started to rotate, thumping faster and faster as they gained speed.

Marvin spoke to someone in the tower, giving coordinates and coded words Isaac didn't understand, and then the helicopter lifted off slightly.

Isaac looked over at Jillian. Her face was pale, but she seemed calm.

The helicopter surged forward, parallel with the ground for several yards, then ascended upward to the blue skies.

No turning back now.

Chapter Seven

Jillian clutched the strap of her purse with both hands. This was pure insanity. What other explanation could there possibly be for running away from home like a scared teenager and somehow ending up on a helicopter – *a helicopter!* – heading out over the Gulf of Mexico? With a man she barely knew.

Yes, it was true, she wanted to know Isaac. From the first time they'd met and he'd dropped an entire sheaf of papers on the floor and tried to shake her hand even though she was carrying a full flat of flowers. He'd been so awkward and cute. But the fact remained that they never spent much time alone together. It seemed like every time he came to Willow Creek, it was to help Summer. Which, yes, helped them all in the long run. And now she was, what? Using him? Not for a fancy vacation at what was surely a very nice place, but as a means to escape her own stupidity.

Marvin's voice came through the headset. "If you look to your right, there's a dolphin pod."

Jillian leaned to the window and looked down. For a split second, her head went woozy from the motion, but she was quickly distracted by approximately two dozen dolphins diving up and down. "Oh, wow."

The sun glinted off their wet bodies as they leapt out of the water and splashed back down into the clear emerald green water.

The pod passed under the helicopter. Isaac watched them out his window. "Amazing, aren't they?"

"I've never seen anything like it," Jillian agreed as she leaned toward his side, trying to catch another glimpse of the dolphins.

When they were out of sight, she took in the view. It was a little disconcerting, being in a helicopter. It didn't feel as safe as being in an airplane, probably because they were surrounded by glass and could see far more than you could see out a tiny airplane window. On the other hand, it didn't feel as unsafe as she'd expected.

The sights were stunning. The water was a brilliant emerald green, and so clear in spots that she could see giant fish going about their business. The sky was a gorgeous contrast, a clear blue with a few puffy white clouds.

They passed over a handful of tiny islands, some big ones, and dark areas underwater that she guessed were reefs. Or sandbars. She really had no idea about ocean floor topography.

She was fascinated by the gentle waves rolling across the surface when Isaac reached over and touched her arm. "We're here." He pointed out his window to an island resort that seemed to rise out of the ocean from nowhere.

Marvin lowered the helicopter to a square asphalt landing pad with a painted white circle a giant letter "H" in the center.

A few minutes later, Jillian stood beside Isaac as Marvin retrieved their bags from the helicopter and a man in white pants and a seafoam green shirt whisked them away. Another man, identically dressed, waited for them at the edge of the helipad with glasses of champagne on a tray. "Welcome, Mr. Frazier. Ms. Sullivan," he greeted with a smile. "I am Corwin. Should you need anything during your stay, I am at your service." He held the tray out slightly toward Jillian.

"Thank you," Jillian said. She didn't really want champagne, but it seemed rude to not take a glass, so she did.

"I'll show you directly to your accommodations. Right this way."

Jillian nearly stumbled because she was trying to take it all in. A hotel rose in front of them, but it was unlike the regular chain hotels she usually stayed in. This one was flawlessly landscaped, and every detail practically flashed money. She was glad their first stop was the room, because she was sweating like crazy in her light cardigan and couldn't wait to change.

The pathways were beautiful white and pink concrete with a treatment to make it look cobbled. Chairs and small tables were strategically placed so guests could sit and take in the views with easy access, but spaced apart and surrounded by yellow butterfly palm plants to afford the illusion of privacy.

But what really caught Jillian's attention were the flowers. Hibiscus in the most brilliant pinks and yellows and reds bloomed alongside more delicately colored plumeria. Bird of paradise and anthurium dotted the landscaping. The scent of jasmine wafted on the salty sea breeze. She was almost disappointed when they reached the end of the sidewalk and Corwin opened the door for them to go inside.

The lobby of the resort was cool, with expensive tile everywhere. Beautiful, and probably practical for cleaning sand that would inevitably be tracked in by the guests. Sleek furniture created a seating area big enough for a dozen people.

Jillian took a step toward the front desk, but Corwin

walked past it, toward a hallway that led to a bank of elevators. Inside the elevator, he swiped a badge and pressed the button for the tenth floor, the highest number on the panel.

She held her purse tight against her midsection, trying to make sense of the sequence of events. Didn't they have to check in? She wanted to ask, but she didn't want to look like a rube, so she stayed silent.

The elevator dinged and the doors slid open. Corwin gestured and said, "After you."

In the hallway, he turned left and led them down a long corridor to a large door at the end. He swiped his badge and pushed the door open.

Jillian had to clench her jaw to keep her mouth from dropping open. This was no ordinary hotel room. She stepped into a large living room. A tiny kitchenette occupied the corner next to the door, and far side of the room was a wall of windows that afforded stunning views of their surroundings. Outside their window was a view of an expansive lawn leading to a strip of pristine beach that disappeared into the water. As if it was a paid actor on staff, not far out in the water, a dolphin jumped out of the water and back in, creating a perfect arc.

Corwin said something about keycards and left.

Suddenly, the view became secondary as Jillian realized she was alone in a room with Isaac. A room they were meant to share. She spun to face him. "This... um..."

He must have understood her thought process. "It's a suite. You'll take the bedroom, of course, and I'll sleep on the couch."

"That doesn't seem fair."

"Trust me, this couch is more comfortable than my bed at home." He handed her a keycard, which she slipped into her pocket.

The couch did look comfortable, but it still didn't seem right. "Don't we have to check in or anything?"

"Corwin did that when we landed. We Fraziers are too precious to do something as mundane as check into a hotel room." He rolled his eyes. "I'll be honest. This trip is always weird for me. We get the superstar celebrity treatment, and it sounds fun, but it's a little unnerving."

"Oh." She looked around the room. Her gaze landed on a doorway. "Is that the bedroom?" She walked toward it without waiting for an answer.

Indeed it was. A massive bed took center stage in the room. A bank of doors covered one wall, and an open doorway on the opposite side of the room led to a bathroom.

"Where do we get our suitcases?"

Isaac's face scrunched a little, like he was embarrassed. "Look in there." He pointed to the tallest door in the wall.

Jillian pulled it open to reveal a closet. Her suitcase sat on the floor, already emptied. Her clothes were on hangers, along with clothes she didn't recognize. "They... unpacked my stuff?" The idea of a stranger going through her suitcase and touching her things was unsettling.

"Sorry. That's how it's done here."

"Okay." She didn't like it, but what could she say?

He glanced at his watch. "It's almost four. We should head down soon."

She tried to call the itinerary to mind but came up short. "For what?"

"Cocktail hour. Casual meet and greet. It should be on the itinerary."

"Right. I haven't really looked at it." She looked down at herself. "Can I change?" She didn't explain that she felt sweaty and gicky after traveling. "It'll only take a minute." She grabbed one of her casual sundresses from the closet and went into the bathroom to freshen up. It doubly creeped her out that her toiletries were out of her bag and placed on the counter and in the drawer. She was not a fan of this level of service. Not one bit.

A few minutes later, they rode the elevator to the ground floor. Isaac seemed tense. He stood stiffly, putting a hand on her elbow as they exited the elevator and walked down another hallway to a door that led outside to a large area with a pool surrounded by a large patio for entertaining.

At the far side of the pool, people congregated around a bar. Jillian's chest tightened. She didn't know any of these people, and she was definitely not in the same league. Heck, she wasn't in the same sport.

Her gaze landed on an older couple who stood a little off to the side, observing. She guessed these were his parents. The woman looked like a female version of Isaac. It would have been nice if Isaac had filled her in along the way, but he seemed on edge himself.

Two kids fighting on the other side of the pool caught her attention. A boy, probably ten years old or so, was grabbing at something wrapped in a blanket, held by an older girl. Jillian guessed she was about fifteen? Sixteen? Fourteen? As she was watching, the plush bundle started to cry.

Horrified, Jillian realized the bundle was a baby. The boy wrenched it from the girl and flung it toward the pool, screeching in glee as the girl screamed. The plush wrapping unraveled. The crying continued as the baby arced through the air and landed in the pool with a splash.

Jillian took two giant steps toward the pool and leaped. Her feet – still encased in her best pumps – hit the bottom of the pool and she sliced upward, catching the baby in one arm as she used the other to stabilize them.

As she surfaced, she turned the baby and... something wasn't right.

The baby was still crying, but the sound began to warble. Mechanical. Electronic. Fading.

Jillian treaded water. Understanding filtered in through the adrenaline. It wasn't a baby. It was a doll. A very, very lifelike doll. Relief flooded over her with a mortification chaser.

The boy was doubled over, laughing hysterically. The girl, presumably his sister, screamed about failing health class.

Nearly everyone else had gone silent, wholly focused on her. A few expressions were disapproving and disdainful. Others were obviously trying not to laugh in her face. She wasn't sure which was worse.

Awesome.

Since ducking under the water and escaping through the drain wasn't an option, she mustered every ounce of courage she had and swam to the shallow end of the pool. Fake baby in tow, she lifted her chin and walked up the concrete steps to get out of the pool.

Isaac rushed to her side.

A sharp voice cracked through the air like a whip. "Charles Frazier-Sheffield!"

The boy's laughter immediately stopped.

The girl was sobbing now. She ran over and snatched the dripping baby from Jillian, then sprinted toward the building and ran inside.

The woman with the commanding voice grabbed the boy by the arm and marched him in the same direction the girl had gone.

Most of the crowd politely went back to their own business while keeping one eye pointed in her direction in case there was more drama.

Isaac put a hand on her back. "Are you okay?"

Jillian swallowed the very last remnant of her pride. "Yeah, I'm fine."

A few feet away, a petite blonde stood, smirking, swirling a drink in a glass. She chuckled softly. "My, my," she said in a deep Southern accent. "We certainly do know how to make an entrance, don't we?"

A brunette rounded the pool with a towel and wrapped it over Jillian's shoulders. "Let's get you dried off." She nudged her toward the door.

Jillian went, flanked by Isaac and whoever this woman was. At this point, she could be a serial killer and going with her was far preferable to standing there while everyone alternately stared and pretended she didn't exist.

Inside, they waited for the elevator. Jillian was acutely aware of the water dripping off her dress onto the pristine tile floor.

The woman said, "Isaac, why don't you go back to the party. I'll take care of her."

Isaac looked at Jillian. "Are you okay with that?"

"Sure."

The elevator opened and the woman ushered her inside and tapped her badge on the panel, then pressed the button for the tenth floor.

Jillian pulled her keycard out of her sopping pocket. "I hope this still works."

"It should be fine. I'm Alexis, by the way."

"Oh. Hi. I'm Jillian. Nice to meet you."

Alexis's arm was still around Jillian's shoulders, holding the towel in place and lending some comfort. "I'm so sorry I didn't have time to meet you before… all that. I was hoping I'd have time to debrief you."

"Debrief?"

The stepped out of the elevator and walked toward Jillian's suite. Thankfully, her keycard worked to open her door and they went inside.

"It sounds kind of dramatic, but it's probably a good idea to know who's who, and I'm completely sure that Isaac, bless his naïve heart, didn't give you a heads up about any of them."

"No, he didn't."

"Well. Let's get you changed and I'll give you the crash course in the Frazier family."

Chapter Eight

Isaac watched the elevator door close. He almost hit the button to reopen it. It didn't feel right to stay downstairs while Jillian went to change, but Alexis was with her. That helped, didn't it? Or did it make it worse, since she hadn't met Alexis until this very moment?

"She okay?"

Isaac turned from his reflection in the gold-colored elevator doors to face Theo. "I think so? Alexis took her upstairs to change."

"Probably a good idea to nip some of the chatter in the bud."

"What chatter?"

Theo inclined his head toward the door. "A certain someone is taking advantage of the situation to cement herself as a more suitable match."

"Oh, for Pete's sake." He let out a heavy sigh and headed for the door.

He strode to the far side of the pool, where his parents stood with Four (his brother), Beatrice (Four's wife), Anthony (his brother-in-law), and, of course, Charmaine Delacorte.

His mother wore a tired, unimpressed expression. "I hope your *friend* is done making a spectacle of herself. At least she pulled this stunt before the entire party was here." She pressed her lips together in a sympathetic smile and touched his arm. "Rest assured, there's no need for you to be embarrassed."

Embarrassed? Isaac stepped back and looked her in the eye. "I'm not." Not by Jillian, at least.

"Darling, she jumped in the pool to rescue a *doll*."

Beatrice huffed a little. "It certainly sounded like a real baby."

"Oh, please. It's a doll for a school project."

Charmaine smirked and said, "Well, at least the outfit she ruined wasn't expensive."

Isaac gritted his teeth and ignored Charmaine. "Jillian thought she was saving a baby's life. That's something to be commended, not ridiculed. Even from you people."

"'You people?' What's that supposed to mean?" his mother demanded.

Theo put a hand on his shoulder and squeezed. "Hey, Mom, I forgot to mention that Gisele sent a scarf to thank you for inviting her. It's an ethically-sourced hand-crafted raw silk thing from Madagascar. Extremely high end. She's sorry she couldn't make it."

She pursed her lips. "I'm sure it's lovely." Her tone clearly conveyed that she had zero interest in a scarf from Madagascar.

"Oh, hey, they're bringing the shrimp canapés around." He nudged Isaac. "Let's go grab some before they're all gone."

Isaac let Theo steer him away from the conversation he didn't want to have with his mother anyway.

They walked around the pool, close to the door, so Isaac could be there when – if – Jillian came back. "Did you really go out of your way to get a silk scarf from Madagascar to keep up the Gisele ruse?"

Theo snorted. "No. I picked it up at Target."

"Nice. No danger of her stumbling across a display of them."

"She wouldn't recognize them if she did. She'll never even take it out of the box."

"Very true." Isaac tried to see through the highly reflective door while Theo relieved a waiter of half the shrimp canapés on his tray.

"These are incredible," he mumbled through a mouthful.

"Was this a mistake?"

Theo shrugged as he swallowed. "I think there are going to be some awkward moments, but I think you'll also have a lot of opportunities to get to know each other better." He popped another canapé into his mouth. "Look. Now you know she rescues babies."

"I really shouldn't have let you do this. I should have come clean and started much smaller."

"Come clean with what?" Charmaine's sultry drawl intruded in their conversation as she approached from the side, exactly where her approach wasn't reflected in the door.

"Go away," Theo said, not bothering to hide a sneer of disgust.

She shot him a glare. "Not a chance."

Isaac ignored her, focusing instead on the people approaching from inside. He brushed past her to open the door when he realized it was Jillian and Alexis.

"Hey, I'm glad you're back. Everything okay? You look amazing." She really did. She'd changed into a different sundress, this one white with yellow flowers and green leaves and vines. Her hair was still clearly damp, but she'd pulled it back into a low bun tied at the nape of her neck.

"Yeah, I'm okay. How much do they already hate me?"

"Well, I sure don't." Theo stuck his hand out to her. "I'm Theo, Isaac's much younger, much more handsome, and much better overall brother."

She cracked a smile at that. "And so modest."

"My humility is legendary." He bent to kiss the back of her hand.

"Oh, please," Charmaine interrupted. "I hope you're not falling for his nonsense." She rested a hand on Isaac's arm, which he immediately pulled away from.

Isaac saw Jillian's expression tighten. She answered, "Not to worry, I'm really good at knowing when someone's fake." She finished with a smile that fit in perfectly with the people she was currently surrounded with. She might be able to handle this crowd better than he'd given her credit for.

Theo covered a smirk while Charmaine met Jillian's smile with a bigger, faker one. She smoothly rounded herself to Jillian's side and tucked Jillian's hand in the crook of her elbow. "Oh, Julian, we're going to be the *best* of friends. I can feel it."

Isaac almost corrected her, but he exchanged a look with Alexis, who stood at Jillian's other side and subtly shook her head. He said, "Charmaine, if you'll excuse us, I have introductions to make." He held out his hand.

Jillian extracted herself from Charmaine's arm and quickly took his hand.

Theo cornered Charmaine before she could object. "I've been meaning to ask you about the Mardi Gras party your parents mentioned."

"Oh, uh…"

Isaac and Alexis whisked Jillian away. Isaac made a mental note to thank his brother later. Talk about taking one for the team.

They walked over to his parents. Four and Beatrice were

still with them, although Beatrice was noticeably hanging back and sipping from her glass instead of engaging in whatever conversation was being had.

Isaac's mother was first to acknowledge their approach.

"Isaac. Darling. And Jillian, I presume. I hope Isaac's assistant was able to get you cleaned up after..." she waved a hand dismissively. "After whatever that was earlier."

Isaac put a hand on Jillian's back. "Jillian, this is my mother, Victoria, and my father, William the Third. He goes by Will. My brother, William the Fourth. We call him Four, and his wife, Beatrice."

Beatrice gave Jillian a warm smile and shook her hand. "It's so nice to finally meet you. If I remember correctly, you're a florist?"

"Yes. I have a flower shop that's kind of set up in conjunction with my brother's bakery and my parents' event venue."

"Ah, working with family. Blessing and a curse, isn't it."

"*Thank* you, Beatrice," Victoria said. "Welcome, Jillian. I hope you enjoy your visit. And not to worry, there will be plenty of time to use the pool." She fake laughed, which was like nails on a chalkboard to Isaac.

Four shook his head. "Welcome, Jillian, it's nice to meet you. And these knuckleheads are the only ones who call me Four. You can call me Bill, which is what the people I like call me."

Will gave a curt head nod in her direction, then checked his watch and said, "Isaac, family meeting at five." He turned and walked over to the bar.

Isaac saw his family with new eyes. Ugh. What a dumpster fire this was. Why had he ever thought it would be appropriate to bring Jillian into this? Especially on short notice with no warning? He really shouldn't have brought her here without some intensive preparation, including spreadsheets and a PowerPoint presentation with flowcharts to let her know what she was getting into.

Now, instead of preparation, he'd have to do damage control to make sure she didn't hate him by the end of this. Lots of damage control.

He hoped Jillian was willing to stick around long enough to see past the obnoxious façade some of his family put on.

And maybe not judge him for their actions.

This was a terrible idea.

Chapter Nine

Jillian kept her head held high under Victoria's scrutiny. Thankfully, it was short-lived because Will clinked a fork against his glass to get everyone's attention.

Apparently a man of few words, he waited until everyone was focused on him, then said, "Family meeting in the main ballroom. Now." Then he headed inside without another word.

Isaac said, "This'll last until dinner. I'll see you there, okay?"

Jillian had no idea when or where dinner was supposed to be, but she nodded and said, "Yeah. No problem. Enjoy your meeting."

"Enjoy? Not likely." He chuckled.

She watched him cross the patio and disappear through the door. A few minutes later, she and Alexis and the bartender were the only ones left.

Alexis inclined her head toward the bar. "Shall we?"

"Sure."

They each got a fruity cocktail and walked to a small seating area overlooking the pool. "Okay, I'll give you the crash course." Alexis pulled her phone out and opened a file of photos. "This is Caroline. She's the mom of the two kids with the doll. The boy is Charles, and the girl is Willa. From what I gather, the 'baby' is one of those super lifelike dolls that they use for health class as a pregnancy deterrent. I don't know about you, but we used an egg in my school."

Jillian chuckled, thinking back to when she'd done the project. "We used bags of flour."

"You met Victoria and Will, Bill and Beatrice, and Theo."

"He seems really nice."

Alexis looked up from her phone and smiled. "Bill and Beatrice are lovely. They're on the Frazier Industries side of the business. Theo and Isaac both work in The Frazier Foundation, which is technically the philanthropic arm of Frazier Industries. Theo's a lot like Isaac. But different. They're both super nice guys. Like *genuinely* nice guys. They're humble and kind to the core. Super smart. Theo's a lot more outgoing and extroverted, and you know Isaac is pretty cautious and laid back. They're really close. Bill is also sort of caught in a middle ground between those two and Caroline." She swiped on her phone. "This is Anthony. Caroline's husband. They're..." She looked skyward, clearly trying to carefully choose her words. "They're more closely aligned with their parents and the company and... all that entails."

Jillian met her gaze, understanding that Alexis was giving her a sort of warning as well as a Cliff's Notes version of the family dynamic. "Got it."

Alexis showed her more pictures with more names, but Jillian's brain refused to hold any more information. "I hope there's not a pop quiz," she drily joked.

"I know it's a lot." Alexis was sympathetic. "I'm really glad Isaac finally got up the nerve to invite you. He's been talking about it at least three years. But I wish his courage had shown up a little sooner than yesterday."

An odd combination of emotions swirled through Jillian.

She was flattered and happy that Isaac had been thinking of her, apparently as long as she'd been thinking about him. But there was a solid flow of guilt that she hadn't accepted this invitation to be close to him. She'd jumped at the chance because it was a convenient way to flee the predicament she'd gotten herself into at the very moment she was desperate to flee.

Why did everything have to be so complicated?

"When is dinner?"

"Six thirty."

Jillian checked her watch. It was a quarter after five. "I think I might walk around a bit. Where will dinner be?"

"I'll show you."

She followed Alexis inside. She pointed down one long corridor to a set of wide doors that were currently closed. "The banquet hall is right there. If you're thinking of walking down to the beach, it's that way." She gestured to a set of glass doors across from the front desk.

"Thanks. For everything."

Alexis waved a hand. "Think nothing of it. I'm here for you for this entire trip. Anything you need." She gave Jillian a wink, then walked away.

Jillian pushed through the door and out into the warm late afternoon air. The breeze coming off the water helped to balance the thick humidity. She made her way across the lawn to a grouping of yellow butterfly palm plants that sheltered two cozy chairs and a small table. She settled onto a chair and looked out over the breathtaking view. Immediately in front of her, perfectly manicured soft green grass that led down a gentle slope to a wide strip of pristine beach with light beige sand that darkened as it merged with the water lapping at its edge. The water was clear at the shore with tiny whitecaps on the rolling waves slapping the beach. As it got farther from shore, it turned brilliant green, then a deep blue-green. The sky was perfectly blue with a handful of puffy white clouds.

She couldn't think of a single better view, but it was hard to enjoy because guilt was eating her up. She felt guilty about the list, guilty about Summer finding it, guilty about running away, guilty about using Isaac to accomplish running away, guilty about swearing Kate to secrecy, guilty about not telling Gavin where she was, guilty about embarrassing Isaac...

Although that one wasn't totally on her. That thing looked like a real baby. It cried like a real baby. How on earth was she supposed to know it was an ultra-realistic doll? Sure, if she'd taken time to assess the situation, she might have realized no one else seemed concerned, but that was only with the benefit of hindsight. She decided to scratch that one from her list of shameful things.

She hoped dinner was uneventful, although guessing from this crowd, there would probably be seven forks to choose from, and she could guarantee she'd pick the wrong one, and his mother would notice.

"Jillian?" Alexis's voice cut through her thoughts. "We should go in."

How was it twenty after six already?

Jillian followed her to the dining room. Isaac stood in the hallway, his face splitting into a huge grin when he saw her.

"How was your meeting?"

He rolled his eyes. "Typical." He put a hand on the small of her back and gently steered her to the far side of the room. He pulled out a padded chair for Jillian, then slid into the seat beside her.

Much to her relief, their other tablemates were Alexis, Theo, and an unassuming older couple that Isaac introduced as a member of the board of directors and her husband. As soon as he said the names, they escaped her mind.

Thankfully, dinner was as uneventful as she'd hoped. There were only two forks, and it was pretty obvious which one was for the tiny starter salad and which one was for dinner. The food was excellent. A brown-sugar-crusted salmon took center stage on a plate with roasted asparagus spears and mashed potatoes.

One server cleared their plates as other servers began to set dessert in front of the guests. The dessert, a fancy take on deconstructed s'mores, was even more delicious than it looked. She savored every bite.

When she was finished, Jillian pulled her cloth napkin from her lap and leaned over to Isaac. She whispered, "I'm going to the restroom. Be right back."

He rose slightly from his chair as she got up.

Clacks from her heels echoed in the empty hallway as she hurried to the restroom and pushed the heavy door open.

The restroom was large and, like the rest of the resort, high end. The long row of stalls boasted expensive full-length doors, which was always a welcome perk in public toilets.

Jillian took the stall farthest from the door. She'd no more than sat down when people came into the restroom.

She immediately recognized Victoria's voice.

"Why he thought it was appropriate to bring *her*, I'll never know. I can't believe she dove into the pool. Right there in front of everyone!"

"Mother, stop." This voice probably belonged to Caroline. "I can't fault her for that. We paid a small fortune for the stupid thing to be realistic, and it certainly was."

"But who would think a fourteen year old would have an actual baby?"

Probably Caroline answered, "Look where she's from. Fourteen is probably on the old side for having a baby."

Rude snickering followed the quip.

Wow. What a bunch of catty mean girls. Jillian leaned forward, squeezing her thighs together so she didn't start peeing and alert them to her presence.

A third voice chimed in with a sultry Southern drawl. "I can only imagine he brought her along to antagonize me."

Victoria agreed. "That makes more sense than him actually being interested in her. Poor thing actually thinks she can get her hillbilly claws into him. You know she's only interested in his money."

"Just let me take care of that," Charmaine purred.

Probably Caroline drily said, "He already dumped you once."

Wait, Isaac and Charmaine had been together? Ugh. Of course they had. It made sense. A lot more sense than Isaac being with her, a florist from Willow Creek.

Stall doors creaked and slammed.

It felt like forever until the three of them finished their business. They kept jabbering, switching topics to the subpar menu and that it was clearly time to make some changes in the kitchen staff until the door banged shut behind them, cutting off their voices.

She waited a beat to make sure she was alone so she could finally pee in peace.

She took her time washing her hands, then steeled herself to be confronted in the hallway, but thankfully it was empty. Instead of turning right to go back to the dinner, she turned left to the elevators and went upstairs to the room. She quickly changed into shorts – low class denim shorts and a t-shirt – and grabbed her hoodie, also low class, then took her hillbilly self back down to the lobby and ducked out the glass door that led to the beach.

It was almost eight o'clock, and the sky was dark. The moon was large and bright, probably two or three days away from being full. Stars dotted the sky. The air was chilly, but still comfortable. Definitely better than the evening temperatures in the forties at home.

She walked across the plush green lawn, past the seating area, down the gently sloping hill dimly lit by small solar lights, to the edge of the sandy beach. She kicked her shoes off and carried them with her to the edge of the water.

The water was freezing cold as it lapped onto the beach and over her feet. Goosebumps covered her legs and arms, but she ignored the cold and walked along the edge of the surf.

Her phone vibrated in her back pocket. She slipped it out of her pocket to check the caller and stopped walking abruptly. Summer. Her feet sank as the water pulled the sand back to the sea.

What a mess she'd made of things. And like most problems, running away from it was making it worse.

The call stopped, and Jillian saw that it was the sixth time Summer had tried to call in the span of half an hour. A moment later, a buzz let her know she had a voicemail.

Correction, she now had three voicemails.

And a string of text messages.

> Where are you?

> I need to talk to you.

> Call me ASAP.

> IMPORTANT. CALL ME.

> HELLO??????

Jillian half-wished she'd have indulged in more alcoholic beverages, because mustering up courage on her own seemed like an impossible mission.

Chapter Ten

Isaac watched his mother, his sister, and Charmaine come back into the ballroom and head back to their table, but Jillian still hadn't returned. He waited five minutes, then five minutes more.

"Please give Jillian our good nights," Lenore said as she and her husband rose from their seats.

"Of course. Have a good evening."

After they left, Alexis said, "Do you want me to check the restroom?"

"Yes, please." He didn't want to be overbearing or creepy or stalkery, but he also didn't want her to be having some sort of stomach issue that could be helped with some Rolaids or ginger ale, either. Although he suspected any sort of stomach issue would have been caused by the trio who'd just returned. And if that were the case, she probably would have texted him or Alexis.

Alexis was back in a couple of minutes. "She's not in there. Do you want me to check the room?"

"No, I'll go see if she went upstairs. Good night."

Theo said, "Let me know if you need anything."

"Will do." Isaac made a hasty exit. He wasn't thrilled to share the elevator car with a handful of other guests, but fortunately they were involved in their own conversation and all he had to do was nod and tell them to have a good night when they got out on their floor.

He pushed the door to their suite open and was relieved to see Jillian's things still in the room mostly undisturbed. He glanced into the bedroom. The dress she'd worn to dinner was draped across the corner of the bed. The bathroom door was wide open, so clearly she'd come back to the room, but wasn't there now.

He crossed the room to look out the window. The soft solar lights along the edge of the beach cast just enough light for him to see her walking along the water's edge. He patted his pocket to make sure he'd grabbed the room key, then hurried back downstairs and across the lawn. He stopped long enough to kick off his shoes, peel off his socks, and roll up his pantlegs.

The top layer of sand was cool, but just underneath was still warm from a day spent baking in the sun.

"Jillian?"

She abruptly turned and walked toward him. "I'm sorry."

He hurried over to her.

"I should have let you know where I was."

"It's okay," he assured her. "Did something happen?"

She sighed and looked out over the water.

"I saw my mother and her crew coming back from the direction of the restroom. Did they say something to you?"

"*To* me? No."

Her answer was confirmation that they had definitely said something. No surprise there.

"This was a huge mistake, Isaac. I'm so sorry, but I shouldn't have come here."

"What did they say?" It didn't take a great leap of imagination to think of any one of the trio saying something so awful it made Jillian want to leave. And the three of them together? Harder to imagine them *not* saying something awful.

"It's not even them. I mean, that's a small part of it, but I shouldn't be here for a lot of reasons. I don't belong here."

"That's not true." He reached out and put his hands on her arms. "I'm glad you're here. I want you to be here."

She sighed again.

"Tell me what's going on. What you're thinking. Please."

"Maybe we should sit down."

Well *that* didn't bode well, did it? Isaac followed her to a mound of sand close to the lawn and sat beside her. She buried her toes in the sand and hugged her arms around her knees.

"I think it's best if I go home."

It took a second to digest the words. "But why?" He shifted to look at her.

"This all came together so fast. I never should have said I'd come, but there are things going on at home... In the bathroom, your mom and sister and Charmaine were talking about how I want your money and I'm using you."

"I know that's not true."

"Well, part of it is."

His neck jerked, stunned by her words. She was after his money?

"Not the money, obviously. And not using *you*, but using this invitation. Yes, I wanted to see you, and I was so excited to hear from you, but the only reason I said yes was because I needed to get away. Like, desperately. Your message came in like a rescue boat and I jumped at the chance, and I feel horrible that my motives for coming here were selfish."

He wasn't sure how to respond, so he said nothing.

"Your mom thinks I'm a low-class hillbilly, an opinion I cemented when I jumped in the pool for a doll."

"She doesn't think you're a hillbilly." His argument was weak.

She gave him a side-eye. "Isaac, she literally said I'm trying to get my hillbilly claws into you for your money. That's a direct quote."

He shouldn't be surprised. Truth be told, he wasn't surprised. Disappointed, yes. But surprised? Not so much. "I'm sorry. For what it's worth, I thought jumping in the pool was brave and selfless. Yeah, it turned out to be a doll, but better to save a doll than stand by and do nothing and have it turn out to be a real baby. You made the right split-second decision, and I one hundred percent support that."

"Thanks."

"Please don't let them chase you away. I'll have a talk with my mother."

"It won't matter. She's made up her mind about me, and she's clearly on a mission to get you and Charmaine back together."

Her phrasing set off alarm bells in his mind. "Back together? We were never together in the first place." He needed to put a stop to that notion immediately. "Never."

"When they were in the restroom, Charmaine said something about taking care of you and your sister asked how that was going to work since you already dumped her once."

Isaac rubbed his eyes with the heel of his hand. "No. I went on one date with Charmaine. One. It's probably been eight years. It was a horrible evening, I ended it early, and we never went out again. There was no 'together.' There was no dumping. One excruciating dinner. That's it. It doesn't matter what my mother wants, I have less than zero interest in Charmaine."

"She's very beautiful."

"So are lions but I don't want to be near one."

That got a chuckle from Jillian. She looked out over the water and said, "There's just so much more going on."

"Tell me about it. Maybe I can help."

"Thanks, but you can't. It's a hole I dug myself into, and I'm the only one who can get myself out."

"Try me. If nothing else, I can help brainstorm solutions. That's kind of my jam." Finding unexpected solutions was the best part of his job.

She let out a long breath, her shoulders drooping. "I'm warning you, this does not make me look like a good human being."

He doubted anything could make her seem like a *bad* human being. "I'm ready."

"I've never gotten along with my sister. Like, ever. I'm almost six years younger than Summer, so I was always wanting to tag along or have things she had or do things she did, and I never could. At some point it turned from a simple age thing to a really ugly, horrible, petty, one-sided rivalry that existed mostly in my own head."

Isaac was surprised because they seemed to get along well enough when he was in Willow Creek, but he could understand where she was coming from. Caroline and Four were the oldest, and had perks and privileges he and Theo didn't.

"I started to blame her for everything and got it all twisted in my head. For instance, I would get so mad thinking about how she went to the movies all the time. Every weekend, and even some weeknights and she forgot all about me. She saw everything that came out and I never did." She lowered her hand to the sand and traced lines with her fingertips. "The part I conveniently ignored was that she worked there. That's just one example from a whole laundry list."

That didn't sound so bad.

"When Summer moved away, it got better. We'd get along

when she came home, but I was always glad to see her leave." She winced, but continued. "Then, when she moved back home to take care of the farm a few years ago, I got really petty and I didn't even realize what I was doing until I got so obnoxious that Gavin had to pull me aside and tell me to knock it off. I had a hard time adjusting to her being home, because, well, you've met Summer. She's so outgoing and friendly and commands whatever room she's in, but in a way that people want to be around her. And when someone like her is in the room, someone like me gets forgotten."

Isaac couldn't disagree more that Jillian got forgotten, but he stayed silent, letting her gather her thoughts.

"Long story short, it was around that time that I realized that the problem wasn't with me and Summer. The problem was with me. Just me. So I started looking for a therapist and reading a lot of self help books and listening to podcasts and all that stuff. It took almost three years to finally find a counselor I really like who also takes my crappy insurance. This leads to my current situation."

"Okay."

"She gave me an assignment. Basically I write down every single thing I ever felt that Summer 'did' to me. Everything. Just brain dump it all onto one list. After I get it all out, the idea is to go through and challenge every item as to whether it was a fact, or a fiction I conjured up."

"Sounds interesting." He was a big fan of pros and cons lists, and this seemed like a similar concept.

"I had the list in my office before the Halloween festival Saturday night. I got called out to fix the flower arch by the bridge and left the list laying out in the open, right there on my desk, and after the event it was gone. The only person who had been in my office was Summer, because she had to grab something."

"Oh. Wow." He cringed in sympathy.

"I panicked and all I could think about was running away. Then you texted me."

He almost used the opportunity to come clean and tell her that it had been Theo who sent the text, but he didn't.

"The last thing I put on the list was being jealous over you."

"Me? What?"

She lifted a handful of sand and let it slowly sift through her fingers. "Long after your business dealings were done, you still put a lot of time and effort into helping her. Getting your legal team to shut down Nina Hardwick and her online attacks was huge. Don't get me wrong, I'm grateful because it helped me and Gavin and of course she didn't deserve any of that, but it made me feel some kind of way that you were so involved with her and once again, I felt forgotten."

Isaac shook his head. "Well, that's one for your fiction column."

"How?"

"Look. Sure, I like Summer. She's a good client, and after all this time, I consider her a friend. But I didn't pull those resources and involve my legal team for Summer. I certainly never forgot about you, Jillian, because I did that for you. All of it was for you. If Nina Hardwick had been able to continue, it would have meant the end of Willow Creek. And then what would have happened to Jilly's Blooms? That's what I cared about. I'm glad it helped your family. But that was all secondary. The most important thing to me was that it helped you."

She looked stunned. "Really?"

"Of course." He wanted to reach over and take her hand, but he resisted the impulse. "Do you know how often I typically revisit the businesses I work with?"

"No. How often?"

"Between zero and one. I'm always available via email or phone, but I can count on one hand the number of businesses I've made the trip back to see in person. I've been back to Willow Creek a dozen times. And that's not so I can help Summer. It's always because I'm hoping to see you."

"I assumed it was part of your regular routine."

"It's not." He looked out over the water and sighed. "It would be a lot simpler if I could be a little more like Theo and just straight up tell you I want to see you."

"That would be a lot simpler."

"I really want to see you."

"I really want to see you, too. So I think the best thing is for me to go home."

He didn't follow that logic at all. "You're already here, though."

"Not for the right reasons." She let another handful of sand sift through her fingers. "I have a whole list of missed calls and messages from Summer. I need to go back home and deal with this face to face before it gets any worse."

He didn't want her to go, but he could understand why she wanted to deal with this in person. "Okay. I'll have Alexis arrange it."

"Thank you, Isaac. I'm sorry. I know it's inconvenient, and I'll reimburse you for the travel expenses."

He balked at the very suggestion. "Absolutely not. You're here as my guest."

"At least your mom will be happy." She gave him a half-smile. "It's kind of ironic that the gardens are full of anthurium."

"What's that?"

She pointed to a nearby plant with large, waxy, heart-shaped leaves and long white stamen covered in pollen. "Those plants. They symbolize hospitality and kindness."

He chuckled. "I'm sure she didn't pick them out." He stood up and held out his hands to help her up. When they were both on their feet, he brushed the sand from his pants as she did the same. "I know you have a lot on your mind, but does this mean we can start over and maybe plan something on purpose?"

"Yes, please." She bent to pick up her shoes, then reached over and squeezed his hand as they walked up the sloping lawn to the resort.

The darkness hid his grin as he wrapped his fingers around hers and she left her hand in his the whole way back to the room.

Chapter Eleven

Had it really only been twenty four hours since she climbed out of a helicopter onto a private island in Florida? The whole thing seemed like a fever dream. It was surreal that it was only Tuesday and she was almost home.

Home. Ugh.

Her stomach churned with anxiety and dread. She was afraid of the inevitable confrontation she was about to have with Summer, but sort of looking forward to getting it over with and out of the way. Hopefully they'd be able to hash it out and move past it and someday, somehow, end up with a good relationship.

It was just after four o'clock when she made her way through the Harrisburg airport to grab her luggage from the baggage claim carousel and make her way through the parking structure to her car.

Her phone vibrated on the passenger seat while she waited in line at the toll booth in the parking garage, and her dashboard lit up, letting her know it was Summer calling. Again.

She felt like a coward, ignoring the calls for the hourlong

drive home, but this really, really, really wasn't a conversation that should happen over the phone.

Instead of heading home, Jillian gave herself a pep talk and mustered enough courage to drive straight to Willow Creek.

It was dark enough that the lights had come on in the parking lot of The Shoppes. Her chest tightened all the way up through her neck. She hated confrontation of any kind, but especially when she was so completely in the wrong and there was no way to defend herself.

Summer and Gavin's cars were still in the parking lot. She slid into a spot a few spaces away from them.

Her hands trembled as she turned the car off and opened the door. Her legs felt like jelly as she took the first step of her walk of shame into the lion's den.

The lobby of The Shoppes was empty except for the scent of gingerbread. Batter Up! was still brightly lit, as was hallway leading up the stairs to Summer's office. The bulbs made a clear path pointing to where she would have to face the consequences of her actions.

She considered ducking into Jilly's Blooms and taking a minute to collect her thoughts, but another minute was a minute too long. She steeled her shoulders and put her foot on the first step.

Her fingers gripped the railing.

Step.

Step

Step.

Her feet moved her upward. With every stair, the anxiety grew. This was going to be horrible, mortifying, humiliating, and there was nothing she could do except breathe and get through it.

The door to Summer's office was ajar, with more light spilling into the hallway.

Jillian's courage stalled at the top of the stairs. Last chance to be a coward and flee back downstairs and hide in her shop. Or home. She could run back to her car and go home.

Which would only postpone the inevitable. And give her an ulcer in the meantime.

She pulled in a long, slow breath, trying to relieve the band of pressure in her chest. Her mind ran through a million scenarios about how Summer would react when she saw Jillian. Would she scream? Throw things? Curse and say horrible things? Or worse, cry? Would her eyes flash anger or hurt?

There were so many ways this could go, and none of them were pleasant. The best Jillian could do would be to stand there, listen to everything Summer said, and beg her forgiveness. Later, when Summer was ready, she could explain what the list was about. Now was not the time to defend herself or make excuses. Now was the time to let Summer say whatever she needed to say.

She took a step forward and the wooden floor creaked like a gunshot. No turning back now.

Another deep breath. She lifted her chin and walked to the doorway.

Summer sat across the room, bent over her desk, writing something.

Jillian lifted her hand and quietly rapped on the door with her knuckles. Her stomach flip flopped.

Summer looked up and jumped to her feet.

Oh, no. Was Summer going to come over and punch her? That was a definite possibility she hadn't considered.

As Summer approached, she tensed, waiting for Summer's fist.

"Where have you been? I've been trying to get ahold of you. Did you get my messages?"

She couldn't speak, so she nodded.

"My goodness, what's going on? Nobody knew where you were. Gavin said Kate said something about Florida and something about Isaac, but he didn't know and Kate wasn't giving any details. Are you okay?"

What was happening here?

Summer continued. "I'm glad you're here. I've gotten two dozen calls, I kid you not, in the past forty-eight hours about the Anderson wedding in a tizzy about the flowers. I emailed you the changes, but I'm guessing you didn't see them. Anyway, come look at this." Summer walked back over to her desk.

Jillian stood in the doorway, confused. Why hadn't she brought up the list? Her legs felt funny when she took a step toward the desk.

Summer flipped a manila folder open to reveal a floorplan sketch for an upcoming wedding they were holding in Creekside Hall. She slid the page over to reveal a second floorplan. "Here's what they originally wanted. There would have been ten tables, which is what they ordered the centerpieces for." She tapped the second sketch. "Here's what they want now, which is twenty tables, which means double the centerpieces, but they want them smaller. I need you to take a look and get me the difference in pricing as soon as you can, if it's even something you can do. I didn't know if you already ordered the flowers."

Jillian blinked stupidly. "That's why you called?"

"Sorry. I know I was psycho calling, but I wanted to hopefully catch you before you put the order in."

Her mind whirled, trying to grasp for information about whether or not she'd already ordered the flowers. No. No, she hadn't. She remembered now. That was on her list for early next week. "Um, no. I didn't order the list."

"Huh?"

"What? Flowers. I haven't ordered their flowers yet."

"Are you okay?"

No, she was not. "I... I thought you were calling about the list."

Summer's eyebrows scrunched inward with concern. "Jillian, do you need to go to the hospital? Are you having a stroke or something?"

"No?" Stroke? No. Floating in an alternate reality? Quite possibly.

"What list are you talking about? The list of flowers? It's all the same varieties of flowers. The centerpieces will be pretty much the same, just a little smaller because the tables are smaller. I don't know much about floral design, so if that won't work, let me know. Maybe we can stagger flower centerpieces with candles or something. Ugh, these people are so high maintenance."

"Oh." This was not computing at all.

"I'm serious. Are you okay?"

She shook her head. "Yeah. I think so. Just a weird couple of days."

"Did you get abducted by an alien or something? Where were you?"

"Florida." She tried to gather her wits. "Isaac invited me to his family resort in Florida and it was really last minute. I only told Kate because I needed to borrow some of her nice clothes because I didn't think my stuff would fit in very well with his family."

Summer's expression changed to sympathy. "Didn't it go well?"

"It was... okay. Different, I guess."

"It couldn't have gone that well if you're home already."

"I came home to get this taken care of." She waved her hand to indicate the folder on the desk.

Now it was Summer who was confused. "You could have just called me back."

"It's complicated." Her mind, and her stomach, started to catch up to the realization that Summer didn't know anything about the list. Thank goodness.

But if Summer didn't take the list, who did?

And what were they planning to do with it?

Chapter Twelve

Isaac sat in one of the Adirondak chairs overlooking the water.

"This seat taken?"

He looked up at Alexis. "No, what's up?"

"I just wanted to check on you. Have you talked to Jillian?"

He checked his watch. "No, she's probably just now getting home. I figured I'd wait a little while to message her."

"I hope everything's okay. I really like her and I hope I get to spend more time with her."

"Me, too."

She lowered her voice. "I need to warn you about something I overheard."

"Oh, geez, now what?"

"Charmaine has a keycard for your room."

"What?" Isaac sat up straight.

Alexis grimaced. "Theo and I were sitting at the pool when Charmaine and your mother came out and I don't know if it was the way the wind was blowing or what, but we could hear every word. Your mom got a duplicate keycard from the front desk and gave it to Charmaine. She's planning to sneak into your room tonight."

"This is ridiculous." The anger rose up in his chest.

"Sorry."

"Don't apologize. Thanks for letting me know. I guess I'll sleep on the grass," he grumbled. "Or get the keycard changed."

She leaned a little closer. "Or you could turn the tables a little bit, if you're up for it."

"I'm listening."

"You could swap rooms with Theo. I personally think it would be kind of hilarious if she snuck in and found him instead of you."

Isaac laughed, loud and hearty. He had not expected that from Alexis. "Diabolical. I didn't know you had it in you."

She chuckled. "It was Theo's idea."

"That makes a lot more sense. I'll have to meet up with him."

"No need." She held her glass up in front of her mouth. "Give me your keycard. I'll switch the rooms. All you have to do is keep an eye on everybody and keep me posted."

"Wow. You're going to leave me for a job with the CIA, aren't you?"

She snort-laughed. "Plot twist. I already work for the CIA and this assistant gig is just a cover."

He slipped her his keycard. "I'd laugh, but I'm not too sure it's a joke."

She just winked and walked away.

Isaac casually strolled out to the courtyard, where his parents milled around, rubbing elbows with their guests. His mother caught his eye and slightly inclined her head to the side, which was her way of summoning him to where she stood.

"Isaac. Darling. It's such a shame your friend had to leave so suddenly."

"Yeah, I'm sure you're really upset about that."

"We were looking forward to getting to know her."

He couldn't contain his eyeroll. "Sure."

"You should spend some time with Charmaine."

"There is no scenario in which that's happening." His jaw ached from the tension making it clench.

"Be a good host, dear. Charmaine is probably bored out of her mind."

"Charmaine is busy scoping out the crowd for her next elderly husband."

"Don't be crude."

"I wouldn't dream of it." He sipped at his ice water. "I do expect you to get to know Jillian at some point. She's not going anywhere." He hoped, anyway.

His mother looked around obviously. "She's not? I must have been mistaken when I saw her leave."

"Funny."

"Darling. She showed you where she stood when she left so unceremoniously."

"She had a family emergency."

"Isaac, I want what's best for you. You're too high-value to settle. You need a partner who understands your lifestyle."

High-value? What kind of ridiculous buzzword was that? "Not a partner who loves me for who I am?"

She hand-waved that notion away. "Love is nice, but what you need is someone suitable, and you clearly can't be trusted to select someone on your own. Aim a little higher than a florist from some no-name town in the middle of nowhere. Even Theo had the sense to chose a doctor."

He quickly took another sip of water to keep from laughing in her face.

"At least we know Gisele isn't after his money."

All humor evaporated with her dig at Jillian. "You think

Charmaine isn't after money? She's already bled three husbands dry and you're desperate to sign me up to be next?"

"She's established and ready to settle down."

"You need to stop with the Charmaine thing. It's not happening. Not now, not ever."

"Don't take that tone with me. You should remember who you're speaking to."

Isaac matched her one-eyebrow-raised glare. "I will. As soon as you remember I'm not a child, and I'm not playing this game with you."

From the corner of his eye, he spotted Charmine sidling closer.

"Did I hear my name?"

Isaac decided to lean into his annoyance. "Yeah. I was telling Mother to stop trying to play matchmaker because there is zero chance of you and I having a romantic relationship. I hope that's clear enough for both of you to understand."

Her face betrayed nothing.

His mother, however, huffed in annoyance.

Isaac picked up the tongs at the breakfast buffet and put a sausage link on his plate. His mother strode across the room, making a beeline right for him, regal and furious.

"What were you thinking?" She ground the words out through gritted teeth.

"About what?"

"You and your brother have *humiliated* that poor girl."

Isaac looked over his shoulder to Charmaine, who sat with pursed lips and narrowed eyes, glaring holes into his back.

"I haven't even seen her."

She hissed, "You know what I'm talking about."

He dropped another sausage link onto his plate and set the tongs down with more force than he probably should have. "Yeah. I do. I know all about the sick plan you two concocted. You've done some messed up things before, but this takes the cake."

"Me?"

"Yeah, you."

"What makes you think I had anything to do with it?"

Isaac said, "You got a duplicate key and gave it to her. That's sick."

She didn't bother denying his accusation. "Sick? That's a bit dramatic, don't you think?"

"Would you be okay with Dad giving a man a key to Charmine's room without her knowledge or consent?"

She looked shocked. "What? Of course not."

Isaac spread his hands, willing her to connect the dots.

He waited a minute, then looked around the room. It was the last place he wanted to be. He was almost to the age of colonoscopy, and he'd rather be there, doing that, than sitting here. It wasn't even a close call.

He finished filling his plate and took it all the way back to his room to eat in peace. At least the day was full of strategic planning meetings, so there wouldn't be much opportunity for his mother to corner him again, and Charmaine wouldn't be at the meetings at all.

Thank goodness. He'd had his fill of both of them and couldn't wait to go home and figure out how to see Jillian again as soon as possible.

Chapter Thirteen

Jillian spent Wednesday morning sketching out new centerpieces that were slightly smaller, but still had the overall aesthetic the client was looking for. She worked up the new pricing for the additional tables and sent it over to Summer, who would get the approval from the bride.

She was still a bit shaky, waiting for the other shoe to drop. There had to be another shoe, because the list was still missing. She'd gone through her entire office, looking in every file folder, every drawer, every nook and cranny that a piece of paper could possibly fit in or under or behind. Nothing.

She could only assume that Summer was biding her time. She was a professional and great at her job, so there was a chance she just wanted to get through the Anderson wedding first and then she'd let Jillian have it. But was she a good enough actress to seem so unbothered last evening?

Maybe someone else had gotten the list and was planning to blackmail her. But who? And why? The possibilities had churned through her mind all night, making sleep impossible.

"Jillian?"

She screeched and jerked backward, her chair slamming

back into the filing cabinet, causing it to wobble ominously. "Gavin!" A folder slid off the cabinet and fell to the floor.

His concerned expression quickly turned to amusement. "Sorry, I didn't mean to scare you." He closed the office door behind him and sat at the chair in front of her desk.

"What's wrong?" It was unusual for him to close the door, so this must be important.

"That's what I'm here to find out. What's going on with you? Kate would only tell me you went to Florida with Isaac, but you're already back home and awfully jumpy. Did something happen with you and Summer?"

Jillian picked up the folder and let her heart slow back to its normal pace. She leaned forward and put her elbows on the desk. "Sort of? Maybe? I don't know."

"Talk to me. It's not like you to take off without letting anyone know what's going on."

"You're going to think I'm completely insane."

He teased her with a shrug and said, "What else is new?"

"I'm serious." She sucked in a breath and told her story rapid fire, hitting all the major points. "So it turns out she was trying to get ahold of me about the Anderson flowers, but I don't know if she's just biding her time or if someone else has the list or what's going on, and I don't know what to do."

Gavin sat back in his chair and shook his head. He looked mildly irritated. "You know, you could avoid an awful lot of nonsense if you'd just talk to people."

"Okay?" Great. The last thing she wanted was a lecture from her brother.

He pointed to his chest. "I have the list."

"What?!"

"I grabbed it when you ran out to fix the arch."

"But you were right behind me."

"I was looking right at it when you jumped up and ran past me, so grabbed it and shoved it in my pocket."

"Why—"

He held up an annoyed hand. "If you ask me why I didn't say anything until now, I'm going to flip your desk."

That's exactly what she was going to ask, but he was right. He didn't have a chance to tell her because they were busy with the arch, then busy with the event, and then she ran off. She asked a different question instead. "Where is it?"

"In my desk drawer. In an envelope. A sealed envelope. So no, there's no chance anybody else saw it."

She nearly wilted with relief. "Thank you."

"You've got to get this straightened out. For everyone's sake. Figure out what you need to clear up with everyone and get it done."

"That's easy for you to say."

"Is it? You think it's been easy being in the middle of all this? It's not."

"I'm sorry." She ran a hand down her face, then reached back and smoothed her ponytail. "I'm sorry I've put you in an uncomfortable position. I never meant to do that."

He leaned forward, meeting her eyes intently. "Was that so hard? If you can apologize to me, you can talk to Summer. She loves you just as much as I do."

That, Jillian wasn't so sure about.

"Do you want to come along over and get your list out of my bakery? I don't like being responsible for it." He softened his words with his trademark easy grin. "It feels like bad luck."

"Yeah." She followed him into Batter Up!, through the spotless kitchen, and into his small office that was very similar to hers. He opened a desk drawer and handed her an envelope.

"Thanks, Gav."

"No problem."

On her way back over to Jilly's Blooms, she ran into her mom, Andi.

"Jillian! Where have you been? Summer's been trying to get ahold of you, and we had no idea where you were. We were worried sick. Why didn't you let anyone know where you were?"

"It's a long story."

Andi crossed her arms and frowned. "I have nothing but time."

Jillian sighed. "Let's go for a walk." Might as well start with Mom.

They left The Shoppes and crossed the parking lot, headed toward the gazebo that overlooked the creek. The weather was perfect for early November. Bright and sunny. Not too chilly, not too warm. Perfect jeans-and-hoodie weather.

"What's that?" Her mother asked, pointing to the envelope.

"This is the bane of my existence." She folded the envelope and slipped it into the back pocket of her jeans before she sat on the bench overlooking the creek.

"Honey, I'm worried about you. You don't seem like yourself lately."

Jillian thought that might not be a bad thing, to not be herself. Maybe being someone else for a minute would be a relief. "I don't know where to start."

Andi reached over and put a hand on Jillian's knee. "Anywhere. Just talk to me."

"Okay." Jillian looked out over the creek, letting the sound of flowing water soothe her anxiety about coming clean. She took a deep breath and spoke, giving her mother a general overview of what she'd discovered about her feelings about Summer, her misconceptions of the past, and the exercise her therapist had recommended. She left out the part about carelessly leaving the list on her desk and Gavin saving her butt.

Her mother listened intently, letting her speak.

"It's not just Summer. I'm getting ready to turn forty, and I know it sounds petty and childish, but it stings that I've never really had my own birthday celebration. It's always tied up with New Year's, or mashed in with Christmas, like an afterthought. Every year there were people at my sleepovers who weren't even my friends because their parents wanted a sitter." She picked at the hem of her sweatshirt. "It's like I never really had anything all my own." She made a humorless laugh-snort. "Exhibit fifty-one, when I was married to Tate I didn't even have a husband all to myself."

"Tate was a cheating jackwagon." Her scowl punctuated the distaste in her tone. "And a liar."

Jillian watched a bird land on the ground, peck a few times, and fly away. "I didn't even get my own middle name." She hadn't meant to say it out loud.

Her mom's brow furrowed in confusion. "Of course you did."

"My middle name is Marie. Summer's middle name is Marie. It's the same name."

Her mom vehemently shook her head. "But it's not. Summer's named after Dad's grandmother, Mary Marie. You're named after my grandmother, Marie Clara. Just like you and your sister, they were both brilliant, wonderful women who happened to be polar opposites. Mary Marie was out marching and fighting as a suffragette and all sorts of other political activism, and Marie Clara – Nana's mom – worked tirelessly behind the scenes as a nurse, growing herbs and making poultices for injured soldiers coming back from World War II and delivering flowers to anyone in the community having a hard time. As you and Summer grew up, it was so clear we'd chosen the right namesakes for each of you. Didn't I ever show you the scrapbooks? I'm sorry if I didn't. I'd have sworn we looked at them a lot when you were little."

Jillian vaguely remembered seeing old newspaper clippings and photos, but the details were out of her memory's reach. "Really? Dad told me one time that it was because he was sleep-deprived put the wrong name on the form in the hospital."

Her mom rolled her eyes. "He was kidding. You know Dad, sometimes his jokes aren't funny. And I'm sorry about your birthday. You're right, it did kind of get rolled into other holiday celebrations. I should have done a better job of making sure you knew your birthday was special." She reached over and tugged Jillian close for a hug. "*You* are special, I hope you know. I don't know what I'd do without any of my kids. You're all so wonderfully different."

Jillian sank into the embrace. "Different, I agree. I'm not sure how wonderful it is, though."

Chapter Fourteen

Wednesday's strategic meeting felt like it dragged on for an eternity, but in reality it ended just after four o'clock, almost an hour ahead of schedule. Isaac closed his laptop and Alexis closed hers.

"Do you want my notes tonight?"

Isaac shook his head. "No." He exchanged smiles and nods with members of senior leadership walking past them to leave the conference room. "I might need something else, though."

"Sure. What's up?"

"I don't feel right about the way Jillian left yesterday. I should have gone with her or something. Maybe I should go to Willow Creek."

Alexis slid her laptop into her bag and carefully said, "Do you mean just show up? Without letting her know?"

"Yeah? Is that a bad idea?"

"Let's think it through."

He knew that tone. It was her patient tone she used when he was rushing into something. "You think it's a bad idea."

"Isaac. You don't want to jump from one crazy whirlwind

situation to another. Wasn't that the point of her going home? So you could slow down and start again on a smaller scale?"

"Partly. I think mostly it was so she could handle her family stuff."

She raised an eyebrow and waited for his brain cells to connect.

"Oh. You're saying I should let her handle her family stuff and not just show up unannounced. Would it be tacky to send her flowers?"

"Flowers? Isaac."

"That would be stupid, wouldn't it? Either I'd be making her make her own bouquet or I'd be giving someone else a sale. No win there. What about one of those fruit basket things? Or a cake? What if I order a cake from her brother to give to her? That could... That would be weird. The fruit arrangement thing is good though, right?" He ran a hand through his hair.

"It's—oh." Alexis stood up straight, looking at a spot over his shoulder. "Father incoming."

Isaac turned and smiled. "Hey, Dad."

His mouth stayed in a hard line. "Isaac. I don't know what prank you and your brother pulled, but your mother is upset. Fix it."

"There was no prank. There's nothing to fix."

His father stared him down like he'd challenged him to a duel rather than make a simple comment to set the record straight.

Isaac glanced at Alexis. "I'll catch up with you later."

"Yes, sir," she said and snatched her bag to her midsection as she made a beeline for the door.

"Do whatever you need to do to keep your mother happy."

If Isaac wasn't the spitting image of his mother, he'd

wonder if perhaps he'd been switched at birth, because his mannerisms were nothing like his parents. Or his two older siblings. Theo was more of a chameleon, able to shift into whatever persona fit the situation. It was a skill Isaac often found himself envious of.

"William, there you are." Reginald, one of the board members approached, clapping Isaac on the back as he addressed his dad. "I've been meaning to ask you about the fourth quarter projections."

"I'll leave you to it." Isaac gave a nod and smile and grabbed his bag to make his escape.

"Wait." William's voice boomed, sharp and commanding.

Even Reginald startled. "Sorry, I didn't realize you were in the middle of something." He looked a bit miffed, but walked away.

William waited until he was out of earshot then focused on Isaac. "You're too old to play these games. Clearly you brought that woman with you as a joke or to make some sort of point. Enough. Man up, settle down with Charmaine, and knock this nonsense off. Men like us have affairs with florists and secretaries, we certainly do not have *relationships* with them. You are a Frazier, and it's high time you start acting like it."

Isaac adjusted the strap of his messenger bag over his shoulder. Talking back to his father was as effective as talking to the clouds, but he was right about one thing – this was enough. "I'm not getting involved with Charmaine. We aren't some European aristocracy where I have a duty to the royal line to keep our blood pure."

William regarded him coldly. "You've been given too much leeway. You forget why you have your comfortable position, and you forget how easily it can be taken away. You *do* have a duty to this family."

Isaac took a breath. He knew exactly how fortunate he was to have the position he did, and he worked hard to always abide by the foundation's mission of service to the community he was working in. "My duty is doing right by the foundation. It does not involve my personal life." It was a ridiculous argument anyway. They acted like he was a wayward prince getting caught with drugs or shoplifting for fun instead of a man who wanted to do his job and live his life.

"Your brother is poised to take over your position and run the foundation. Unless, of course, you'd like to reconsider."

"Reconsider what? Charmaine?" And Theo was willing to take over the foundation? What was happening?

"Aristade and I are very interested in strengthening our business ties."

Charmaine's father was in on this, too? This whole situation was so gross. As much as he disliked Charmaine, she didn't deserve to be treated like a piece of meat to sweeten some business deal. Yuck. The patriarchy was alive and well.

"Do you have any idea how medievally out of touch you sound? This is completely unhinged." His argument was ignored.

"You have twenty-four hours to make your decision." William strode away, letting the words hang in the air.

Isaac stood in the empty room for a minute, processing what just happened. Trying to, anyway. His father just threatened his job. And for what? So he could be more closely aligned with the Delacortes?

A door at the far side of the room opened, and the worker who came through saw him and froze.

Isaac lifted a hand, trying to convey "No, it's okay, come in." He shook his head once and left the conference room.

The elevator was thankfully empty. He rode up to his floor,

keeping his head down. The doors opened to a couple of people waiting to get on. He kept his eyes fixed on the floor and slid past them.

"Isaac?"

His gaze snapped up to Alexis's face.

She reached out and grabbed his upper arm. "Oh, my goodness, are you okay? Come on." She steered him toward his room, but he stopped abruptly in the middle of the hallway and spun to face Theo.

"Were you going to tell me?"

Theo stepped back, stunned. "Tell you what?"

"That you're ready to take over the foundation."

Confusion bloomed across Theo's face. "What are you talking about?"

Isaac immediately felt horrible. "It's not you then? Waiting in the wings to take my job?"

Theo nudged Alexis's shoulder, hurrying her to get the door open. As soon as it swung open, Theo put an arm around Isaac and ushered him inside to the sofa. "You'd better start from the beginning."

When Isaac was done recounting his story, Theo and Alexis wore matching dumbfounded expressions.

"This whole thing is so bizarre," Theo said. "You and I are the only Fraziers working in the foundation, and Four is dedicated to Frazier Industries. I can't see him moving."

Alexis suggested, "Could he have meant Anthony?"

"Maybe? He's at Frazier Industries, too, but I guess that's the only thing that makes any kind of sense at all."

"Ugh," Theo said, making a face. "When did he start calling Anthony our brother though?"

"If I may make a suggestion?" Alexis said, a little timidly.

"Of course."

"Perhaps it was deliberate, to make you assume he meant Theo. I don't want to accuse anyone of sowing discord, but..." She let the words hang.

"That tracks."

She glanced at her watch. "You might want to head down for dinner."

"I don't want to, but I will," Isaac grumbled.

Theo agreed, following him to the door.

Isaac rode the elevator with them, dreading each ding of the passing floors. He was in no mood to be around his parents, or Charmaine.

The dining room had an odd vibe when they walked in. People talked in hushed tones, whispering and surreptitiously looking around.

"What's going on?" Theo whispered.

"No idea."

They sat at the closest table, which was already occupied by two other people.

From the front of the room, a man got to his feet and clinked his fork against a glass. "May I have your attention, please?"

"Who is that? He looks familiar," Isaac said quietly.

Alexis said, "Alan Henderson. He's been on the Industries board forever."

As soon as she said the name, Isaac knew she was correct.

The room hushed, waiting to see what Alan had to say.

"I'm not a young man," Alan began with a wheezy laugh. "But I recently met a woman who makes me feel like I'm back in my sixties." He wheeze-laughed again.

"Oh, no," Alexis breathed.

"Miss Charmaine Delacorte, you are a breath of fresh air. A ray of sunshine lighting up the twilight of my life."

Isaac sat up taller to see better. Charmaine sat in the seat beside Alan, fluttering her eyelashes demurely.

"I haven't had time to shop for a ring, but I hope you'll still consider having me. And you can shop for the biggest, shiniest, fanciest diamond ring you want as soon as we get back home." He leaned down, attempting to get on one knee, but ended up awkwardly sitting on the edge of his chair, with his leg bent back under the seat. "Charmaine, my beloved. Will you make me the happiest man in the world? Will you marry me?"

"Of course I will!" Charmaine drawled, reaching out to put her arms around his frail shoulders.

A single clap was heard from the middle of the room, followed slowly by another hesitant clap, then another, until an odd sort of polite applause smattered across the room.

Charmaine and Alan stood and waved to the room, then made their way through the tables. Charmaine held Alan's arm, probably more to support him from falling than any show of affection.

As they passed by, Charmaine smirked triumphantly and hissed to Isaac, "You missed your chance."

When they were out the door, Theo snickered and said, "You dodged a bullet."

"You're not kidding."

"Oooh, Alan's daughter does not look happy," Alexis whispered, inclining her head toward the front of the room where Rue Henderson – who was old enough to be Charmaine's mother, if not grandmother – sat stock still with her lips pressed tightly together.

"I hope he gets a prenup," Theo joked.

Alexis shook her head. "Not a chance. They'll probably be on a flight to Vegas before we get dessert. Hopefully Rue already has everything locked down after Alan's health issues last year."

"Let's hope," Isaac said.

Isaac's mother strode over, regal as ever, and gracefully leaned toward his ear. "Obviously we won't expect you to take up with Charmaine right now. But you represent the family. The florist still is not an option for you."

Chapter Fifteen

Jillian woke Thursday with a headache and a to do list a mile long. She hadn't heard from Isaac, so it was safe to assume they were back to where they'd been before the ill-fated trip. Which was… nowhere.

It stung a bit, but she couldn't blame him. He'd invited her on a trip and she'd bailed less than twenty-four hours in. She didn't even want to think about how much the business class plane tickets cost.

In some ways it had been good, though. At least they'd had a few minutes to talk and she knew it wasn't all in her head that there had been something between them all this time. Had been. She doubted the tenuous connection they'd shared was going to survive the hot mess they'd just gone through. Especially after she admitted her petty issues with her sister. And the way his family clearly hated her so thoroughly. There was no way around that when he was so close with them.

She was tempted to reach out to him, but that felt desperate, so she didn't. In the shower, she mentally went through her to do list. She was at the flower shop before eight, working in her office for about an hour when the electronic chimes went off, alerting her to a customer.

She left her seat and went out into the shop, her customer service smile firmly in place. A young man in a delivery uniform stood at the counter, holding a white box.

"Hi, can I help you?"

"Yeah, uh, are you Jillian?"

"I am."

He placed the box on the counter. "Can I get you to sign for this?"

"What is it?" she asked as she took the clipboard. The label clearly had her name and address, so she signed and handed it back to him.

"I'm not sure. Have a great day." He turned and left.

Jillian looked at the box. There was no branding or return address. She lifted the lid and let out a surprised, "Oh!"

Inside the box was a basket full of small clear boxes of fresh fruits and cheeses, all wrapped in pink cellophane and tied with pink ribbon. A card was taped to the top of the box. She peeled it off and opened the envelope.

Jillian,

Since it would be silly to send flowers, I'm sending you a fruit and cheese bouquet instead to let you know I'm thinking about you and I can't wait to see you again.

Isaac

She couldn't help but smile.

"Whoa, what's that?" Summer asked as she came into the flower shop.

"Isaac sent me a fruit and cheese basket since it would be silly to send me flowers."

Summer chuckled. "No offense, I know you love flowers, but give me fruit and cheese any day."

"You'll get no argument from me. It all looks so fresh, too." She pulled the basket out and set it on the counter. "There's even an ice pack at the bottom of the box. This is really nice."

Summer leaned over to inspect the logo printed inside the box's lid. "Oooh, this is the place that did the charcuterie boxes for that birthday party last month. Those were adorable, too."

"I didn't expect this. I haven't even heard from him since I left."

"Is he busy with the business stuff? Didn't you say there were a couple days of strategic planning meetings or something?"

"Yeah, but there's a lot of downtime, too."

"He's with family, though. You know how crazy that can get when you've got the whole gang in one place."

"True."

"Speaking of which, Mom said you needed to talk to me?"

Jillian's heart skipped a beat. She wasn't ready to have this conversation with Summer. "Did she say why?"

"Not really. She said something vague about us needing to hash some things out? Do you know what she's talking about?"

Jillian took a breath. "Yeah. Do you have a few minutes?"

"Of course." Summer's brow furrowed in concern.

Jillian motioned to the wooden table at the back of the shop, where she sat to arrange bouquets. They each took a stool on opposite sides of the table.

"This is awkward and weird, so please bear with me."

"Sure."

"You know I've been seeing a therapist."

"Yeah." Summer leaned forward, listening intently. "Has it been helping?"

Good question. "I think so. One of the things we've been working on is my perception of our relationship."

Summer's eyebrows shot up. "Ours? You and me?"

"Yes. Mainly the tension and conflict we've had over the years." Jillian picked at the strings on her apron. "It's frustrated me that we didn't have the kind of close relationship I always assumed sisters should have. But a lot of that is because I've had some very unrealistic expectations, and, frankly, a pessimistic view. I've been learning that I've put up a lot of walls that prevented us from being closer."

Summer nodded. "I would love to have a closer relationship with you."

"One of the things I need to do in order to be able to move forward is to reexamine the things I felt were unfair or slights or things that made me feel like I was forgotten and left behind."

"Like what?" She cocked her head, fully engaged in the conversation. It was one more piece of evidence that her memory was faulty, and that Summer wasn't dismissive and uncaring.

"It's silly stuff. Like I was so mad that when we were kids you went to the movies all the time, and it wasn't until recently that I remembered it was because you worked there. I was so jealous, but I completely forgot that it wasn't just a fun thing you were doing."

Summer smiled. "Definitely not fun. I swear I can still smell the burnt-on fake butter from cleaning out the popcorn machine."

"I was jealous that Mom and Dad gave you a car and I had

to buy my own. But I conveniently forgot that it was Mom's old, paid off car, and you had to haul me and Gavin all over the place for school and sports and whatever activities we were in."

"And pay my own insurance and gas."

"Exactly. So what I've been working through is reframing the things that I was holding onto and being more honest about how things really happened."

Summer shook her head. Her long brown ponytail swung behind her shoulder. "I'm not sure I'd call it dishonest, Jillian. You were seeing things as a, what, ten-? eleven-? year-old when I was sixteen? I can see where you'd think I was hanging out at the movies all the time or that I got a free car. I hope you're not beating yourself up about those things."

Hot tears stung the backs of Jillian's eyes. "It's not so much the individual things I'm beating myself up about. It's the amount of resentment and nastiness I've allowed to fester all these years, when I think the heart of the matter is that I always felt so invisible. So forgotten. That's always been in my head. That I'm utterly forgettable. Gavin was always so good at sports and you were good at everything and I was good at reading books and planting flowers."

Summer's lips pressed in a sympathetic smile. She reached over and put her hand on top of Jillian's. "I'm so sorry. I guess I always wrote it off as a simple personality clash. I didn't know you were struggling, and I should have."

Jillian shook her head. "No. That's on me, too. Maybe not when I was twelve, but I'm almost forty. At some point it became my responsibility to deal with my feelings and stop holding onto the past. And stop making snarky comments every chance I got." She turned her palm upward and squeezed Summer's hand. "I'm sorry. I haven't been a good sister to you. I... I even blamed you for helping Tate have an affair because on some level it was easier to believe you hated me enough to let him use your apartment in Chicago than it was to believe I was such a bad judge of character that chose a slimeball for a husband." Shame welled up in her gut. Saying it out loud highlighted how absurd it was.

Summer's face scrunched up. "He really is a slimeball. And I'll admit, I was so angry and hurt that you believed I would have helped him cheat on you."

That was more than fair. "I don't think I ever truly believed it, deep down. He had me doubting everything about myself. He really did a number on my self-esteem that took a long time to repair."

"Slime. Ball. He's not worth another thought."

"I know. I'm glad he's long gone." Jillian figured that was a sufficient list of grievances to explain the bulk of the tension between them. "I also told Mom that a big part of why I always felt forgotten was because I never had a real birthday party. It was always rolled in with New Year's or Christmas and the worst one was when I turned sixteen and we were all supposed to go snowtubing, but instead we spent the day getting you and Gavin packed to go back to college."

"Ouch. I'm feeling a little selfish, because I honestly never thought much about how annoying it must be to have a birthday on a major holiday. By New Year's, everyone's partied out and thinking about how to get back in the regular groove. That must have been so frustrating and hurtful to not feel like you had a special day all to yourself."

"I know it's silly."

"Stop. It's no sillier than Dad collecting all his Eagles stuff or Ben making up songs about the cats. Even if it is silly, so what? Life is hard and complicated and we all need to find joy where we can. It's not silly to feel hurt and ignored and want people to recognize that. I'm sorry I didn't, and I will do better."

Jillian's throat constricted. Summer understood? Just like that? And all these years, Jillian assumed everyone – especially Summer – would think she was being stupid and petty and childish. How many other hurts and frustrations could she have avoided by just saying what she wanted or needed? Gavin was right. She needed to learn to talk to people instead of running away or letting things fester and poison her relationships.

She wanted to say something, but the words clogged behind the lump she couldn't swallow down. Her eyes welled. She tried blinking fast to stop them from coming, but it was no use. Tears streamed down her face.

Summer hopped off her stool and came around the table to wrap her arms around Jillian's shoulders.

Somehow, it made Jillian feel even worse. All these years she'd painted Summer as the villain, and here she was, giving comfort and understanding and apologizing for her part in what Jillian had explained.

Taking stock as forty rapidly approached was discouraging when she fell so terribly short of the person she wanted to be.

Chapter Sixteen

Isaac was grateful Thursday was a "free" day. No meetings, no scheduled activities. Since he had exactly zero desire to run into his parents and listen to more of their delusions of royal-lineage grandeur, he jumped at the chance to join Theo on a tiny charter fishing boat excursion.

Alexis said she was itching to spend time on the beach with a novel, so they parted company in the lobby.

The captain of the boat navigated them out into the water and set them up with poles and bait, not that either of them really wanted to fish. The day was brilliant blue, with gentle seas and a steady breeze that rocked the boat with a pleasantly hypnotic rhythm.

Isaac sat back in his chair and propped his bare feet up on the railing on either side of his pole. Theo did the same.

"What are you going to do?" Theo asked.

"Whatever I want. These demands are unhinged and absurd. I'm not entertaining either one of them."

"I'm sorry the trip was a bust for Jillian."

"Me, too. I think it was a mistake to invite her. I should have started smaller."

Theo snickered. "You should have started *at all*."

"That's fair." He lifted his arm to check his watch. "Hopefully she gets the fruit basket and likes it."

"Fruit basket? Why didn't you just send flowers like a normal person?"

Isaac lowered his sunglasses to give Theo a look. "Flowers? To a florist?"

"Oh, yeah. Good point."

"I'm shocked you missed that, Mr. Smooth Ladies' Man. Gisele would be so disappointed." He conveniently left off the part where it had been his first impulse.

Theo laughed. A moment later, he cleared his throat. "Soooo, what's the story with Alexis?"

Issac immediately said, "No."

"What?"

"She's amazing and I need her. Besides, she thinks you have a serious girlfriend working in Galapagos or wherever."

"I told her about the whole Gisele thing."

Whoa, that surprised him. "You did? When?"

"Last evening after dinner. We ran into each other on the beach and we were talking about how ridiculous it was that Mom and Dad think they can dictate who you're in a relationship with. We kept talking and I kind of told her the whole story about Gisele."

Isaac studied Theo's profile. "Alexis is solid. She's genuine and honest and I trust her with my life. I also think she's too good to be dragged into a shitshow of a family like this."

"That's the only thing giving me pause, to be honest." Theo turned to look at Isaac with a little smirk. "Because—"

In unison, they said, "—money doesn't buy class."

Isaac looked back out over the water and sighed. "Not here, Theo. Not now. I don't want Alexis pinging Mom's radar while we're on their turf."

"I don't either," Theo agreed. "You'd be okay with me asking her out when we get back home, though?"

Isaac shrugged one shoulder. "You're both adults. Not much I can do about it." He thought about how that sounded. "I wouldn't have a problem with you asking her out. I *would* have a problem with there being drama and losing the best assistant I've ever had in my career." He lifted an arm and pointed at Theo. "I'd have to kick your ass."

Theo laughed, loud. "You could try."

"Don't underestimate me." There was zero chance Isaac could best his brother in a physical altercation. Theo was muscular and athletic. Isaac was... not.

"Never."

They sat in silence for a while, ignoring the occasional tug on one of the fishing poles.

Isaac posed a question to his brother. "Do you ever feel like you're in the wrong place? Like you don't belong?"

"In general, or with our family?"

"Family, mostly. Did they always act like this and I'm just now realizing it? Or have they ramped up the obnoxiousness?"

Theo thought about it before he answered. "Both, I think. It's easier to think it's not so bad when we spend so much time away from them. We've also got the distance of being in the foundation, so we're not tangled up with them in the day-to-day business stuff."

"That's true." Isaac thought back to the last time he'd seen his parents before the masquerade party. It had been about five months, at their Memorial Day barbeque, where they were busy playing hosts and didn't have time to micromanage his existence. "I want to get out of here. Now. I'm going home." He leaned forward to get up so he could tell the captain to take them back and he could book a ride off the island.

Theo reached over and grabbed his forearm. "Nope.

You're going to sit through tonight's dinner and smile and pretend everything's fine. Then you're going to leave tomorrow afternoon as scheduled. Once you're on the plane, *then* you can start having thoughts and ideas." He pulled his sunglasses off and turned his entire body to emphasize his seriousness. "Keep your mouth shut and get your ducks in a row."

Isaac slid his own sunglasses off to meet Theo's intense stare. "Is this the voice of experience? What are you up to?"

"Me? Nothing. Nothing at all." He popped his glasses back on and leaned back in his seat. "But I'll give you a call tomorrow night when we're away from here and we can talk. About nothing."

Isaac stared in disbelief. Was Theo making moves to leave the company? How long had this been going on? Why?

"Are you heading back to Houston?" Theo asked.

"New York. I have some new clients I'm meeting new Watkins Glen on Monday, so I figured there was no sense in going back to Houston first. You?"

"Cheyenne."

"What's up there?"

Theo half-smirked. "It's more about who's not up there. I knew this trip would test my patience to its limits, so I scheduled my departure accordingly. My buddy has a ranch with 'spotty cell service.'" He made air quotes around the words. "It'll take a week to decompress after this. I'm going to use the time to figure out how to avoid going home for the holidays."

Isaac grinned. "Easy. You're joining Gisele in the arctic. Tagging penguins or something." He glanced at his watch. "Speaking of decompressing, this has been great, but if we don't get back…"

"I was just thinking the same thing."

Isaac put the poles away while Theo let the captain know

they were ready to head back. All too soon, the engine roared to life and they were speeding across the water to the island.

They were too late to sneak into dinner and get situated out of the way. Instead, they were summoned to the "family" table, while Alexis used her lowly position as support staff to avoid the whole mess in favor of room service and finishing her book on her room's balcony.

Isaac wished he had that as an option.

His parents not-so-subtly seated themselves between him and Theo like they were unruly children. Isaac sat with his mother on one side and their older sister Caroline on the other.

Caroline took a sip of her wine and said, "Anthony needs to meet with you. Discuss some of the standard business continuity procedures at the foundation. See if anything needs updated or whatnot."

That confirmed his suspicion that their brother-in-law was angling for his position. But why? Anthony had a cushy office job in Frazier Industries. There was no way Caroline would be okay with Anthony traveling and... He froze with his water glass halfway to his mouth as sudden realization crashed over him. They were going to shift the focus of the foundation. There had been rumblings over the years about shifting to a more straightforward model of fundraising and distributing the funds because it was less work than working with small businesses and doling out grants piecemeal.

All of which may be technically accurate, but Isaac knew from his great-great grandmother Wilhemina Frazier's writings that she would not approve. Her entire mission was boots on the ground. In fact, she probably wouldn't be thrilled with the level of corporateness that currently existed in the foundation that bore her name.

Why hadn't any of this been brought up during yesterday's strategic meeting?

A carefully plated filet mignon was set on the table in front of him.

"Thank you," he absently said to the server.

Theo was so right. Something was off, and he knew he wasn't going to like it when he figured out the details. It was time to round up his ducks and get them in formation.

Chapter Seventeen

Jillian woke up on Friday feeling lighter and more optimistic than she had in a long time. She hadn't realized exactly how much it was weighing her down to put off talking to Summer. Now that they'd talked, she felt so much better. Summer had been so understanding and kind and even apologetic, while not giving Jillian a pass for her uncharitable behavior.

Definitely not the villain.

For the first time in, well, ever, Jillian felt like they had a good chance of building the kind of close sisterly relationship she'd always wanted. Hopefully it would eventually be easy and full of goodwill like her relationship with Gavin.

The morning passed slowly, as Fridays typically do. She sat in her office, researching upcoming trends in wedding flowers.

"Jilly? You here?" Her mom's voice rang out from the front of the shop.

"Yeah, in my office," she called back as she got up and went to the main room. "I didn't hear my buzzer."

"I don't think it went off."

"That's weird. It's been acting up lately."

"I'm taking the facility manager to Rosie's Diner. If you want to come along, you can let her know to get it looked at."

"Heck yeah, let me grab my coat."

A few minutes later, Jillian climbed into the backseat of their mom's SUV.

"What's the occasion?" she asked when they were all buckled in and on the way.

"I was super hungry for one of their turkey clubs."

"And as soon as she said that, I got a hankering for their hot roast beef," Summer added.

"I didn't have time to prepare. Maybe I'll get the—"

"Grilled chicken salad with ranch," her mom and sister shouted out in unison.

"Wow," she laughed. "Just for that, I'm going to order something different."

"And give poor Sandy a heart attack?"

Jillian laughed again. She could imagine their favorite waitress being confused. Half the time she wrote Jillian's order down without asking what she wanted, because it had been the same exact order for too many years to count.

Lunch was more relaxing than Jillian expected. It was something of a revelation to be sitting with Summer and not be tense, thinking about what Summer must be thinking or how Summer must be judging her. What was that saying? "You wouldn't care so much about what other people thought if you realized how seldom they did?"

There was a lot of truth in that. For someone who always felt forgotten, it was actually freeing to realize Summer probably wasn't thinking about her at all. And she certainly wasn't wasting any mental energy plotting ways to live her life in order to make Jillian feel inferior.

"Are you going along? Jillian?"

Her mother's voice snapped her out of her thoughts. "Huh?"

"Nana. Are you going along when we pick her up from the airport tomorrow?"

"Oh. Sure. What time is she getting in?" Jillian couldn't wait for Nana to be home.

"I think eleven fifteen."

Summer shook her head and took a sip of her soda. "I still can't believe she flew to Ohio. It's so close."

"Your dad offered to drive her out and pick her up, but you know how stubborn she can get."

"Nana? Don't be silly," Summer joked.

Jillian laughed at that. "Stubborn? No way."

Sandy came by their table. "You ladies want pie? We have a fresh apple crumb that's still warm."

"Heck yes," Andi said.

Summer and Jillian both agreed.

A few minutes later, they were all leaning back in their booth, making claims of having eaten too much.

"Gavin should do more pies," Jillian said.

"Oooh, I should ask him to make some of those fruit tart things he made for my wedding. I wonder if he'd make some for Thanksgiving."

Their mom sat upright. "Uh oh. I still need to get a turkey."

"I thought Kate was making dinner this year?"

"No, she wanted to make Christmas dinner so I said I'd take Thanksgiving."

Summer cocked her head. "Are we having it in the house or in Creekside Hall? If we're using the hall I'll need to put it on my schedule so I have time to take care of the linens between events."

"Let's see."

Jillian's mind wandered a little as her mom ticked off the

expected guests on each finger. How did Isaac celebrate Thanksgiving? His family didn't seem like a warm, homey bunch. She knew she shouldn't judge based on her very limited interaction with them, but it was hard not to compare what she'd seen of his family with her own.

Was his parents' house full of carefully curated décor, with nothing out of place, where a speck of dust wouldn't dare take up residence? (Or if one did, would someone get fired?) Did they ever just relax and laugh and not worry about appearances?

The trip to the island was so surreal. She knew Isaac's family was rich, but she didn't expect it to seem like he didn't fit in with them at all. He was so warm and friendly and unassuming, where it felt like his family was measuring and calculating with each glance they cast her way. Maybe he was the oddball in his family, like she always felt she was in hers.

"Jilly? You still with us?"

She gave her head a shake and gestured to her empty plate. "Pie coma. Actually, I was maybe thinking of possibly inviting Isaac to Thanksgiving since Kate's not hosting, because I wouldn't want to spring an extra guest on her."

"Oh, but you'll spring one on me?" Her mom joked.

"What does he usually do for Thanksgiving?" Summer asked.

"I have no idea."

"Of course he's more than welcome. Invite him."

Summer agreed with their mom. "Isaac's great. Just warn him about the football frenzy."

"Oh, no," Jillian groaned. "The Eagles are playing on Thanksgiving this year."

"Yuuuuup," their mom sighed. Their dad was a huge Eagles fan and everyone knew it. From preseason in August until the Super Bowl in February, football was his favorite topic of conversation.

The more Jillian thought about it, the more she liked the idea. If he could invite her to a major family thing out of the blue, she could invite him to a major family holiday thing out of the blue, right? Right.

Chapter Eighteen

It was easy enough to avoid everyone on Friday, right up until Isaac wheeled his suitcase off the elevator and into the lobby.

"There you are."

"Caroline." Isaac leaned over and let his sister air kiss a spot in the vicinity of his face.

"We haven't set up a time for Anthony to sit down with you."

"I'll handle that when I get back to the office."

"Why doesn't she handle it now?" Caroline raised an eyebrow and inclined her head to the left.

Isaac looked over his shoulder and smiled at Alexis, who had just gotten off the other elevator.

"Alexandra, I need you to schedule a meeting next week."

"Okay, sure." Alexis ignored the name and pulled her phone out of her pocket.

"Make it Tuesday at ten."

"I'm sorry, Mr. Frazier only has availability Thursday afternoon next week."

Caroline's eyes widened in annoyance. "You misunderstand."

Isaac intervened. "No, she's right. I'm meeting several new clients next week, so my schedule is pretty solid. How about I give him a call Monday evening?"

"Unacceptable."

The steady thump-thump of the helicopter landing gave him an exit from the conversation. "Shoot, that's us, we have to go. I'll text Anthony. It's not like there's any rush." He gave his sister a one-armed impersonal hug and turned to Alexis. "We'd better hurry."

"Yes, sir," she answered and made a beeline for the door.

He followed close behind and didn't stop until they were seated in the helicopter with their headsets on and the doors closed.

"What's going on?" Alexis asked.

"I'm not sure, but I'm going to need you to tie up some loose ends for me. I have a feeling something's about to go down, and I'm not going to allow any of my small businesses to get caught up in it."

"Of course."

Marvin piloted the helicopter off the pad. They all made small talk about the occasional dolphin and the beautiful weather for the twenty minute flight. Soon after they landed, Isaac and Alexis were in the back of a limo, on their way to the airport.

She worked on her phone, fielding emails, while Isaac made a list of things he wanted to check before his meeting with his brother-in-law. His first priority was making sure all of his clients' current grant applications were being processed.

His next priority? Figuring out what the heck was going on with the foundation.

He made a quick to do list and emailed it to Alexis. "I just sent you a list, and I'll probably add more things to it over the weekend, but please don't worry about any of it until Monday."

She glanced up from her phone. "No problem. Did you want me to contact your brother-in-law to schedule a meeting?"

"Thanks, but I'll handle that myself."

They arrived at the airport. The driver got their suitcases from the trunk and a minute later they were on their way to security.

"Have you talked to Jillian?"

"No. I'm calling her as soon as I get to New York, though. I hope she liked the fruit and cheese basket."

Alexis grinned. "If she didn't, let her go. I don't know any woman who wouldn't love a cheese basket. And the fruit, I guess, but mostly the cheese."

"I hope you're right."

She stepped forward as the TSA agent motioned for her. "When have I ever been wrong?"

Isaac chuckled to himself as he waited his turn. Third priority? Making sure Alexis's job was secure.

They parted company. Alexis headed to the closest Starbucks to fuel up for her flight to Houston, while Isaac went directly to his gate.

His plane landed in Albany at five forty, right on schedule. His breath made clouds in the rental car as he waited for it to warm up. The stark contrast in weather was a welcome change that highlighted the fact that he wasn't in Florida anymore. He couldn't wait to get to his condo and shower the day off and relax.

It was almost seven when he finally settled on the couch in cozy jogging pants and a t-shirt with a freshly delivered pizza. He put the television on for some background noise while he ate.

He stretched his legs out and propped his feet on the coffee table. It took a few minutes before he wondered why he hadn't gotten any calls or texts. He tapped to unlock his phone and immediately realized he'd left it in airplane mode. He switched it off and immediately got notifications for several missed calls and at least a dozen text messages, one of which was from Jillian.

> Hope your trip went well. Did you make it home?

He nearly dropped the phone as he fumbled to respond.

> Home safe and sound. Are you busy? Can I call you?

Instead of an incoming text, his phone vibrated with an incoming call.

"Jillian, hi."

"Hi. How was your flight?"

"Uneventful except that I forgot to take my phone off airplane mode, so I've been home for two hours and just now realized I hadn't been getting any messages."

"I wanted to thank you for the fruit and cheese basket. It was so cute. Did you think of it, or did Alexis?" Her tone was teasing.

"It was all me. Well, mostly me. My immediate thought was to send you flowers, but Alexis looked at me like I was stupid and then I thought of sending you a cake, which was also kind of weird, and then I landed on fruit, and when I went to order it they suggested the option with fruit and cheese and I figured, hey, who doesn't love cheese, right?"

"It's really good cheese, too. Six different kinds. Very bougie."

"That was the goal. Bougie cheese."

"Seriously, though, thank you. I love it."

"Good. I was hoping you would." He grabbed the remote and muted the television.

"How was the rest of your trip?"

"It was… interesting." He hadn't even processed everything, so he wasn't sure how to put it into a coherent order.

"Uh oh. That sounds bad."

"It wasn't bad. Just weird. My brother-in-law wants to meet with me about foundation stuff. I'm not sure what he wants to talk about, so it's got me a little on edge."

"Hopefully it turns out to be nothing."

"I hope you're right. Is everything okay with you? Did you get to take care of the important family stuff that was weighing on you?"

"I did, and everything's good. Summer and I had a really good talk."

"How did she feel about the list?"

"Thankfully, she never saw it. Gavin grabbed it and put it away before anyone else could see it."

"That's a relief."

"You're not kidding. I was so happy I thought I might throw up."

"I'm glad it worked out." He waited a beat to make sure she was done with that thread of conversation. "I'm working in New York for the next few weeks. I was thinking I might make a pit stop in Pennsylvania after I meet these clients."

"That's convenient, because I was going to invite you to Pennsylvania in almost exactly two weeks."

"Really?"

"Yeah. I was wondering if you'd like to come for Thanksgiving. I mean, I'm sure you have your own family traditions and I'm not trying to make you—"

"Yes." He cut her off. "I would love to come for Thanksgiving."

"It's a whole family thing. Everybody will be here."

Nothing sounded better. He could easily imagine that a Sullivan holiday would be warm and chaotic and loud and fun and relaxed. Basically the polar opposite of his own carefully curated family holidays. "Even better."

"We're having it at the farm."

"Perfect."

"Really?"

He settled back against the couch cushion. "Was I supposed to say no?"

"What? No. Of course not. I wouldn't have invited you if I wanted you to say no."

"I wasn't sure you'd want to see me again at all after you met my family." The second the words were out, he wanted to pull them back.

"Why would you think that? I'm the weirdo who embarrassed you by jumping in the pool."

He needed to set that straight. "You did *not* embarrass me. Not one bit."

"Your parents certainly seemed embarrassed enough."

"What they think is irrelevant."

"Is it though? I would think it's important that your family approves of who you're with. Not that you're with me, which I'm sure is a relief to them. I mean, your older brother's wife is an attorney, your sister's husband works for the family company, and your younger brother's girlfriend is a doctor that travels the world helping people. Then you show up with a florist from Nowhere, Pennsylvania."

"First of all, my parents don't exactly approve of my brother-in-law. They tolerate him because he's willing to do whatever they tell him to. Second of all, Theo's girlfriend doesn't exist."

"What?"

"Yeah. Theo got so sick of our parents and their ridiculous overinvolvement and opinions on his personal life that he sort of created Gisele. Apparently he went on one date with her, but they didn't vibe."

"At least he did date a traveling doctor."

"Nope. She's an accountant or stockbroker or something like that. Theo made up a whole backstory and keeps his fake girlfriend overseas to keep our parents off his back. He even sends gifts to Mom from Gisele."

"Oh, my."

"And it's about to get complicated because I'm pretty sure he has a thing for my assistant."

"Ooooh, Theo and Alexis? I can see it."

"Really? It seems so weird to me. I guess because Alexis and I are so close and Theo's my brother and it just seems... weird."

Jillian's laugh rang in his ear. "I can sort of understand that. Ben's been like an extra brother since we were little kids, so when he and Summer finally got together it was a little bit of an adjustment. Although I guess for me and Gavin it just made it official that he was our brother."

"I guess." He wasn't convinced.

"Tell me about your new clients. What are their businesses like?"

Isaac was glad to switch gears away from talking about his family, and ended up talking her ear off about his upcoming whirlwind of meetings with half a dozen small businesses.

Talking with her was so easy and comfortable. He kicked himself for waiting so long. And kicked himself again because the reality was that if Theo hadn't grabbed his phone and made the first move on his behalf, he wouldn't be talking to her right now.

Chapter Nineteen

Jillian's phone beeped. She pulled back and looked at it. "Oh, shoot, my battery is at two percent. I guess I'd better go before it goes completely dead."

"Let me know the details of Thanksgiving. I'll probably come down Wednesday evening if I can find a room."

"Perfect. Good luck with your meetings next week." Her phone beeped again.

"Sweet dreams, Jillian."

"You, too." She wanted to say something else. What, she wasn't sure, but it didn't matter because her phone shut down.

She could hardly believe they'd been on the phone for two hours, talking like they had these conversations all the time. It was so comfortable and easy and she couldn't wait to do it again.

Saturday and Sunday flew by in a flash. After they picked Nana up from the airport Saturday afternoon, the whole family spent most of the weekend letting her regale them with tales of her adventures in Ohio, which included a massive family reunion with her cousin's husband's side of the family and a trip to a seniors' line dancing competition. In which

Nana and her partner placed third. And just like at home, Nana got herself thrown out of a bingo hall. Not her fault, of course.

Jillian stayed close by, enjoying the happiness that radiated from Nana as she told her stories.

Late Sunday evening, Jillian, her parents, Nana, Summer and Ben, and Gavin and Kate sat in the living room. Dad kept stealing glances at the football game muted on the television. Gavin stretched and stood up. "I hate to rush off, but I've got an early morning."

That set off a domino reaction until everyone was on their feet and heading to the door except Jillian. Her dad escaped to the basement to watch his game in peace, and her mom went to the kitchen.

Nana hugged everyone and watched out the door as they drove away. Then she came to sit beside Jillian on the couch and patted her knee. "How have you been?"

"Good. Everything's going really good right now." Having Nana back home made everything even better.

"I was worried about leaving you here by yourself."

Jillian wasn't sure what she was talking about. "I wasn't by myself. Mom and Dad were here. So was everyone else."

"Yes, but I meant by yourself without someone to stick up for you."

The back of her neck prickled. "What?"

Nana squeezed her knee. "You know. To be a sort of buffer between you and your sister. When I was in Ohio all I could think about was how me and my sister are so much like you and Summer. Agatha is so domineering and bossy and it was hard for me to hold my tongue sometimes, but I have to so I don't make her mad."

An unpleasant slideshow spun through Jillian's mind, highlighting times over her life where Nana had tried to be a buffer between her and Summer. She meant well, to be sure, but maybe instead of being a buffer, she'd inadvertently been a wedge.

The thought stung. Immediately she tried to find reasons why that couldn't possibly be true, but now that she'd had the thought and subconsciously run it through the filter of whether it was fact or fiction, she knew it was true. There was no doubt that Nana's intentions were pure. She loved Summer, and that wasn't even a question. But maybe in trying to protect Jillian, she'd gone too far and hadn't let her work out her differences with Summer naturally.

"I'm glad to be home and back in your corner."

Jillian put her hand over Nana's and ran her thumb over Nana's soft skin. "There's no need for corners. Summer and I had a good talk and worked out a lot of our differences. We're in a really good place."

"That's good, I suppose."

"It is." She could sense some tension from Nana, so she changed the subject. "I have news."

"Oh?"

"Isaac's coming for Thanksgiving."

"Why?"

Jillian did not expect that response. "Because I invited him."

"Obviously, but why did you invite him for a family holiday? That's something for a serious beau, not a business associate." Nana's expression soured.

"He's not coming as a business associate, and he's not a serious beau."

"What is he then?"

"I don't know, exactly, but we're figuring it out."

Nana slid her hand to her own lap and pressed her lips together in disapproval. "I don't see why he needs to be included in a holiday then. That's for family."

She didn't bother to argue that they'd included various friends and neighbors and one year even complete strangers who'd gotten a flat tire. Her dad had run out to grab milk at the only open convenience store and saw the couple stuck along the side of the road, so he helped put their spare tire on and then brought them along back home for dinner. Nobody had batted an eye.

"I hope he doesn't turn out to be like That Other One." Nana refused to use Tate's name ever since the divorce.

"You've met Isaac plenty of times. He's a very nice man."

"That you know of."

She wasn't sure where any of this hostility was coming from, so she decided to chalk it up to being tired from her trip. She stood and straightened her sweater. "It's getting late. I'll see you tomorrow." She leaned down and kissed Nana's forehead. "I'm glad you're home. Love you."

"Love you, too." Nana smiled up at her.

Jillian went through the kitchen. Her mom sat at the table, reading a magazine. "I'm heading home."

Her mom stood up and cast an odd glance toward the living room. She whispered, "That was weird."

"I thought so, too," Jillian whispered back.

"Not that I was eavesdropping, but it's hard not to hear."

"I know." She reached over and gave her mom a hug. "See you tomorrow."

Monday was chilly and damp. Jillian took her laptop upstairs to Summer's office to go over the final order for the Anderson wedding. She heard a voice as she got close, but the door was open, so she peeked in.

Summer saw her immediately and waved her in. She

pointed to the phone in her hand and rolled her eyes. "Yes, of course. No problem at all."

Jillian quietly settled herself in the chair across from Summer.

"Of course. Yes, I'll take care of that for you. No, no problem, we want everything to be absolutely perfect. Of course." Her tone was placating. "Mmhmm, we'll talk soon. Have a great day." As soon as she hung up, she groaned. "Tablecloths. Apparently the Anderson bride was scrolling through our Instagram and found pictures of these shimmery gold tablecloths, so now instead of the tablecloths she had reserved, she wants white cloth tablecloths with the shimmery gold see-through cloths on top. Or maybe the black cloth base. She's not sure. She'd like to see them both, so I'll be the good little planner and go set up two tables and send her pictures. She's driving me bananas."

"Good timing then. I'm here to go over their flowers before I finalize the order. Do you want me to get the mockup centerpiece so they can see the flowers with the tablecloths?"

"Genius. Yes." She pushed back from the desk. "Do you mind if I go do that now?"

"I'll grab the centerpiece and help you."

"You're the best. I'll meet you in Creekside in five."

Jillian grabbed her laptop and headed back to the flower shop while Summer went into the storage room to grab tablecloths.

A few minutes later, they worked to set up a round table in the corner of the room in Creekside Hall. After they put the table up, Jillian went to the kitchen to pull place settings while Summer put the tablecloth on.

"I'm excited Isaac is coming for Thanksgiving," Summer said as she fluffed the gold shimmery cloth out and arranged it.

"Me, too."

"I have to admit, I'm a little surprised you invited him. I thought you'd chicken out."

Jillian laughed. "I thought I would, too." She recognized that a year ago, she would have assumed Summer was making an insulting dig at her instead of gently teasing. It felt so, so good to finally be in a comfortable place with her sister.

"What's going on with you two?"

"I have no idea." Jillian set the plates on the table.

"What do you want to be going on with you two?"

She shrugged one shoulder and carefully placed a fork beside a plate. "I really like him," she said quietly.

Summer stopped working and straightened. "He really likes you, too. That much is super obvious."

"We're so different, though."

At that, Summer laughed. "You're more alike than you think. You're both patient and reserved and kind and methodical and highly intelligent." She went back to working on the table settings. "You're just like Jane and Bingley."

"You mean from *Pride and Prejudice*?"

"Yeah."

"Oh, so we're minor side characters?" Last year, she would have honestly bristled at the reference. Now, she was curious what it meant.

Summer stood straight and put a hand on her hip. "What? No. First of all, Jane and Bingley were the main characters in their own story. Second of all, who would Lizzy have been without Jane? Or Darcy without Bingley? Jane was Lizzy's anchor. Without her, Lizzy would have ended up running off when she was fourteen like Lydia did, or worse, married to Collins, just to escape. Ick. And without Bingley, Darcy never would have ended up at Netherfield at all, and he most certainly wouldn't have gone to the ball, so he never would have met Lizzy."

"What does that have to do with me and Isaac?"

"Simple. Isaac is absolutely Bingley in every sense. He's rich, which is nice, but hardly the point. He's good and kind and helpful, but romantically shy. He loved Jane from the moment he saw her and that was it." Summer nudged Jillian's arm. "Just like when Isaac first saw you."

Jillian felt her face heat as she smiled. "I don't know about that."

"And you're so Jane. Reserved and beautiful and strong and capable, with deep emotions that tend to stay hidden. Calm in a sea of chaos."

Was that really how her sister saw her? She'd rattled off the list without hesitation, and obviously believed those were positive traits. Once again, Jillian was reminded how much time she'd wasted, and for nothing. She had to blink back sudden moisture in her eyes.

Summer had thankfully turned back to the table. "Okay, I think that's good. Let's place the centerpiece and I'll get a picture." She took pictures from several angles, then made a face. "I wish I could do that magician thing where you whip the tablecloth out from under everything without knocking it all over."

"That would be a useful skill, for sure." Jillian helped her move everything and swap out the white tablecloth for the black one so she could take more pictures to send the bride. "I think I like it better with the black."

"Me, too. It really makes the gold pop, and brings out the orange in the flowers."

They worked side by side to get everything set up, then neatly put away.

"What does Isaac's family usually do for Thanksgiving?"

Jillian walked alongside her on the way across the wet lawn on their way back to The Shoppes. "I didn't ask. After I invited him, we got on other topics and I never circled back around to ask." She bit her lower lip, then said, "Nana doesn't seem happy he's coming."

"What? Why not?"

"I'm not sure. When I told her he was coming, she said Thanksgiving is only for family."

Summer's face scrunched. "Well that's crap. Do you remember the year Dad brought those people home from the convenience store? They were complete strangers."

"That's what I was thinking. You don't think... Does she not like Isaac?"

"If she doesn't, she's nuts because he's great. She's probably just exhausted from her trip and not acting like herself. I bet once she gets some rest she'll be glad he's coming."

"I hope so."

They crossed the parking lot. Summer grabbed the door and held it open for Jillian.

"Thanks."

"Thanks for helping. Let's get this flower order finalized before she decides to make more changes to that."

Chapter Twenty

The drive from Isaac's condo to Watkins Glen was too far to commute each day, so he grabbed some fast food and settled into his hotel room.

In some ways, his nomadic lifestyle suited him. He loved going to new places, meeting new people, and getting to see how differently everyone chose to operate their businesses. Many times he was able to help streamline and improve procedures, and there was a significant number of times he learned something himself that he could pass on to his clients.

In other ways, it was tiring and lonely to not have a solid home base to go back to. Yeah, he had his condo, which was his and he did like it a lot, and he had the apartment in Houston, but that wasn't any more homey than a hotel room.

He wanted a happy medium. A nice house to come home to that was his, that had his clothes in the closet and maybe a lawn to mow and a garage to tinker in.

Now *that* was a dream. If Isaac tinkered with anything in a garage, he'd probably lose a finger because mechanical stuff was definitely not in his wheelhouse.

He could have a solid home base and still travel.

Then again, this line of thought could be all for naught, depending on the direction the foundation was going.

He finished his food and resigned himself to making the phone call to Anthony, who answered on the second ring.

"Anthony, it's Isaac," he said unnecessarily. "Caroline said you wanted to talk to me." As he said it, it was even more ridiculous. Anthony was just as capable of making a call as he was.

"Hey. Yeah. I wanted to get with you to talk about the business continuity stuff. Basically get a look at everything you do so if we ever had to repla—uh, if you needed, um, like, if you left or, uh, took an extended, uh, vacation, um, to keep everything, um, running smooth."

"Really." If Isaac had been suspicious before, he was ten times more suspicious now.

"Um, yeah. We're, uh, updating the procedures and stuff."

"Why are *you* dealing with continuity for the foundation?"

Anthony sputtered a bit. "Uh, my role is, um, I'm overseeing some, uh, disaster plans. It's just, um, standard stuff."

"I'm just trying to understand why there's crossover since you work for Frazier Industries, which is a completely separate entity from The Frazier Foundation."

Anthony's voice was tight and wheezy. "They just want some stuff streamlined. It's all legit and totally above board."

They who? There was nothing about this that was legit or above board. Isaac switched tactics. "What do you need from me?"

"Uh." It sounded like he hadn't expected any sort of cooperation.

Isaac continued. "My procedure manual is already on the foundation intranet under the exec files. I assume you have access to that."

"Uh."

"Why don't you take a look at that and then let me know if you need me to update it or if there's anything that's unclear."

"Yeah, uh, well, um, what I actually need is more like the day to day stuff."

"My procedures cover all my day to day stuff."

"Um, specific stuff, like contact information and schedule and all that stuff. Like, what clients you have in the pipeline."

Isaac still couldn't parse exactly what was going on, but the writing was definitely on the wall. He figured the easiest thing to do right now was buy some time. "Yeah, no problem. I've got a full schedule of meetings this week, but I'll work on getting it all together and get it to you probably mid-week. Oh. Wait. That's Thanksgiving. How about the Monday after Thanksgiving? That's probably the soonest I can get everything together, but that shouldn't be a problem since this is all just for backup and continuity purposes, right?"

After an uncomfortably long pause, Anthony said, "Right! Yeah, I was thinking sooner just so I can get this all wrapped up, but you're right. Totally right. Yeah. The Monday after Thanksgiving will be fine! I, uh, I guess I'll see you at Thanksgiving dinner then?"

"No, unfortunately I'll still be in New York."

"Bummer." Anthony's voice was sheer relief.

Isaac almost felt bad for him, because he was one hundred percent sure that he was just a pawn in one of the ever-present schemes going on behind the scenes in the Frazier family.

Almost.

But not quite.

As soon as they hung up, Isaac called Theo and filled him in on the odd conversation.

"Do you have any of your client contacts in the intranet?"

"Yeah. I have my calendar and contacts stored there so Alexis can access them as well."

"Do you have them in your own files?"

"What do you mean?"

Theo patiently spelled it out for him. "I mean if some weird IT glitch were to corrupt those files, can you access your own information?"

"Oh. Yeah. For sure. I have everything on my laptop because a lot of the areas I visit have spotty internet access."

Theo sighed. "Please tell me you have another backup."

"Not really. Do I need one?"

"Isaac, for the love of all that is good in this world, do you never listen to me? If it's not backed up, it doesn't exist."

"It's backed up on the intranet." He was feeling a little dense, like he was missing something Theo was trying to convey.

Theo's voice sharpened. "I need you to listen carefully."

Isaac snapped to attention. "Okay."

"First thing tomorrow morning, you're going to the nearest store that sells electronics and you're going to get an external hard drive."

"Okay."

Theo started to explain what he should look for, then abruptly stopped and sighed. "Send me your address."

"Why?"

"Just do it."

After Isaac texted his address, there were several minutes of silence. "You still there?"

"Yes. I just scheduled a delivery for you. It was easier than leaving it in your hands. I'll send a cashapp request so you can pay me back."

Isaac smirked at the phone. "I'll just take it off your tab."

"You know how to back up your files, right?"

"Of course." He wasn't a complete technical idiot.

Theo changed topics. "What do you think is going on?"

He propped his feet on the coffee table. "I wish I knew. I'm guessing they're going to put Anthony in charge of the foundation and change the mission somehow."

"Just a heads up. I'm not going home for Thanksgiving, so you'll have to do your own recon."

"I'm not going, either. Jillian invited me to have Thanksgiving with her family."

"Whoa, that seems like a big step. Things must be progressing."

"Not really. I already know everyone, so it's not like it's some big Meet The Parents thing."

"Does this mean you two are official?"

"I'd say no. We haven't had a conversation about it, so I don't want to make any assumptions."

"But you want it to go that way."

"Of course I do." He wasn't telling Theo anything he didn't already know.

"Can you see yourself staying in one place? Like making a home base for real?"

"Yes. I can." He took a deep breath, then let his thoughts turn into words. "Maybe it's time to step away from the family business."

"Maybe start your own small business consulting firm?" Theo suggested.

"I'm not sure how I'd work out all the logistics."

"You'd scale back and start as a regional operation to begin with. Go through and cherry pick your best clients since you don't have any kind of non-compete contract. You know that's what they were hinting at during the strategic planning session."

"Yeah, that caught my attention."

"You've got the most solid business ethics of anyone I've

ever met, Isaac. But use those ethics to build something for yourself."

"It's kind of overwhelming. I don't know how to start."

Theo snorted. "Yes, you do. It's literally what you coach people to do, all day, every day."

He wasn't wrong. Isaac looked up at the ceiling. All day, every day.

"Let's have a sit-down after Thanksgiving. You and me. We'll have our own strategic planning session."

Isaac sat up and put his feet on the floor. "Are you saying we should do this together?"

"I'm done with it, bro. I was always more comfortable having you and me in the foundation while Four and Caroline worked the 'real' business. But something's going on behind the scenes and I don't like it. I can't quite put my finger on it, but I think they're going to start using the foundation in ways that are going to have great-great grandma Wilhelmina rolling in her grave and I want no part of it."

The relief that coursed through his veins was sudden and unexpected. It was so reassuring to have Theo put words to the feelings he'd been having. "Are you sure you're actually ready to make a move though? You've got a pretty cushy position, too."

"My resignation letter's already written. I'll hold onto it until you're ready to make the leap."

"What about you? Are you really ready to have a home base?"

There was a long pause. "I guess I should have told you. I'm not sure why I didn't. My buddy's ranch up here in Cheyenne?"

"Yeah?"

"There's no buddy. It's my ranch. I bought it five years ago and if I'm not in Houston, I'm here."

Isaac's excitement deflated. "Cheyenne's a long way from the East Coast."

"Yeah. But if I'm not traveling to Houston, I can be traveling to the middle of nowhere, Pennsylvania, instead."

That made a lot of sense.

Before Isaac could say anything else, Theo said, "Give it some thought. Do some of those fancy planning worksheets you have your clients fill out. We'll talk after Thanksgiving."

Chapter Twenty-One

Jillian put the last sprig of greenery in the centerpiece she'd created for the Thanksgiving table. Her mom and Nana were no doubt in the kitchen, cooking enough food for an army.

Thanks to a last minute oven malfunction, Kate's parents were added to the guest list. Cheryl and Roger's turkey was currently in the oven in the Creekside Hall kitchen, and would be carved for leftovers.

Jillian stood back and inspected her centerpiece from every angle, turning it this way and that. The sunflowers were perfect. Bright and cheerful, their splash of yellow reflected the flower's meaning: joy and happiness and thankfulness, which was extra appropriate for the occasion. Satisfied with the placement of the flowers, she carried the centerpiece from her flower shop to the house.

The smell of deliciousness rolled over her like a warm wave as she stepped in from the chilly outside. All the scents mingled together. Turkey, gravy, potatoes, sweet potatoes, corn, stuffing, and a pleasant faint undertone of lemon from the dishwasher as it whirred to clean the second load of dishes for the day. The chatter and laughter from her mom, Nana,

Cheryl, Kate, and Maggie was a comforting sound that warmed Jillian's heart.

"Where do you want these?" she asked.

"On the—Oh, those are gorgeous, sweetheart. They'll go on the table. Or maybe the sideboard? Can you put one extra leaf in the table? We should probably do that before—" Andi wiped her hands on her apron and turned toward the dining room.

"Mom, I've got it." She went to the dining room and set the flowers on the sideboard. The brown and rust-colored plaid tablecloth was already on the table. Jillian folded half of it over and reached under the table to undo the clasps.

"Need a hand?" Summer asked, coming in from the living room.

"Yeah, thanks. Mom said to add one of the leaves."

Summer rolled her eyes. "We're adding all three."

"Good call." They worked together to pull the table sides apart to reveal a wide space, then carefully set each of the three two-foot leaves into place, lining up their slots and notches. Once those were in place, they pushed the table back together to close any gaps, then turned the clasps underneath to lock the leaves into place.

"Gorgeous flowers."

"Thanks. I feel like it's too small, but I knew the table would be full, so I restrained myself."

"I'm not sure I could have. Those sunflower petals are the perfect shade of yellow."

Jillian touched one of the flowers. "I almost ordered chrysanthemums instead. I'm glad I didn't."

"Is Isaac here yet?"

"He should be here any minute."

Summer pointed at each chair as she counted. "Mom, Dad, Nana, Gavin, Kate, Maggie, Lucas, Ben, Me, You, Isaac."

"And Roger and Cheryl," Jillian added.

"Ah. Lucky thirteen."

"Fourteen!" Maggie stood in the doorway, beaming at her phone. "Darian is coming."

Jillian and Summer exchanged a look. "Who's Darian?"

"My boyfriend. We met at college. He's studying nursing."

"Good for him," Summer said. "Just make sure to seat him away from Nana or she'll try to make him look at her bunions."

Maggie made a face. "Eew. Please tell me she won't do that."

Jillian nodded. "She will."

"One hundred percent," Summer said.

The doorbell jangled. Maggie ran off to answer and came back a minute later looking a little disappointed, with Isaac in tow.

"Hi!" Jillian rushed over and gestured to the large slow cooker he was carrying. "What's this?"

"Heavy. Where should I set it?"

She ushered him into the chaos of the kitchen. "Set it here." She made space on the counter.

"Isaac, I'm so glad you could come," Andi said. "You didn't have to bring anything."

He shrugged one shoulder and gave her a shy smile. "It's warm spiced apple cider. I thought it might go well with dessert."

Nana lifted the lid and inhaled deeply. "It smells wonderful."

"Thanks. Mrs. Peabody was making a huge batch for the bed and breakfast, and it was so good I wanted to make some myself. I figured it was more appropriate than a bag of chips."

Maggie squealed as the doorbell jangled again. A moment later, she pulled a nice-looking but quite hesitant young man into the fray of the kitchen.

Introductions were made, but Jillian was certain the poor boy wouldn't remember anyone's name.

"Okay, everybody out!" Her mom waived her raised arms toward the doorway. "Shoo!"

"Uhhh, any chance we can squeeze two more people in?" Ben asked.

"What happened?"

"The more, the merrier," Andi answered over her.

Jillian grabbed two more chairs and shuffled the ones already circling the oblong table.

Summer grabbed more plates as Ben explained.

"Jenna and George and the kids all have food poisoning. She told Mom to come pick up the food, but Mom didn't want to risk it in case it was something contagious."

Jillian paused in rearranging the chairs. "Aren't they in Florida?"

Ben said, "They moved back a couple weeks ago. Mom and Dad said they were going to find a restaurant."

"No, no, no," Nana said, shaking her head. "That's no way to spend Thanksgiving."

"Told you we needed to put all three leaves in the table," Summer muttered with a smile.

"TOUCHDOWN!" their dad yelled from the living room.

"Turn that television off!" Andi shouted from the kitchen.

In response, he cheerfully sang, "Fly, Eagles, fly."

Jillian finished with the chairs and looked around the room until she spotted Isaac, leaning against the doorframe between the living room and dining room. He wore a peaceful smile in the midst of all the noise and chaos. She wondered what he was thinking.

"I should have warned you," she said as she approached him.

"About what? This is awesome."

She raised a skeptical eyebrow. "Is it like Thanksgiving with your family?" She assumed not.

"Not even close."

She wanted to follow up and ask what his family holidays looked like, but Ben's parents arrived and there was another wave of activity that ended with everyone heading for the dining room, except Mack and Gavin and Ben, who were tasked with carrying the bowls and trays of food from the kitchen to the table.

"I can squeeze in here between you," Nana said at Jillian's side.

"Of course."

"Just so nobody makes a scene."

It took several beats before Jillian realized Nana was positioning herself between her and Summer. The realization unsettled her, but that was something to ponder later.

Everyone sat and the men put the food on the table. Murmurs of how delicious the food looked and smelled, and how beautiful the centerpiece was flowed around the table.

Lastly, Mack set the platter of carved turkey on the table and looked to Andi. "Are we missing anything?"

She scanned the table and made a move to stand. "Salt and pepper."

He motioned for her to sit while he retrieved them from the kitchen. He came back with the shakers and took his seat at the sort-of head of the table, then held out his hands on either side.

The sixteen people seated around the twelve-person table joined hands while he said grace. After the "Amen," the room was immediately filled with the sound of silverware against dishes as bowls were passed.

A few seconds in, their mom's tinkling laugh floated over the table. "Clockwise," she said as she redirected a bowl so everything was passed in the same direction.

From there, the dishes and the conversation flowed smoothly. At the first lull, Nana said, "Who wants to start?"

Isaac looked at Jillian questioningly.

Normally it would be Summer who spoke up for the benefit of their newcomers, but this time, Jillian took the lead and spoke a little louder than normal so everyone at the table could hear. "Nana's talking about our Sullivan family Thanksgiving tradition. During dinner, we go around the table and say something we're grateful for. It can be anything, big or small."

From the far end of the table, Maggie said, "I'll start. I'm thankful Dad and I were able to get all those cupcakes decorated and delivered to the food bank yesterday. And I'm thankful Darian was able to come for dinner." She nudged him.

He smiled and blushed a little. "I'm thankful to be here, of course, and I'm thankful this semester is almost over."

Lucas hurried to swallow a mouthful of food. "I'm thankful Dad and Trish are finally getting married."

Maggie added, "Me, too."

Kate said, "I'm grateful for picking up a new client."

Gavin beamed with pride beside her. "Not just a new client. A new *team* of clients. She's going to be doing meal plans and prep for an entire pro hockey team."

A round of congratulations could be heard.

Gavin continued, "I am also thankful that Maggie and I got the cupcakes done for the food bank yesterday. And in that vein, I'm thankful the food bank is here and providing such a wonderful service to the community."

Ben set his fork down and took a sip of water. "I'm sorry my sister and her family aren't feeling well, but I'm grateful they moved back to Willow Creek. It's so nice to have them close."

Andi said, "We'll fix them some meals so they can eat when they feel better."

"I appreciate that," Ben answered. He nudged Summer. "Your turn."

Summer said, "I'm thankful for my sister."

"Wow. I guess I'm chopped liver," Gavin joked.

"You smell like chopped liver," Summer fired back.

Nana pressed her lips together disapprovingly as everyone else laughed.

Jillian said, "Your turn, Nana."

"I'm just thankful to be here. I'll probably be gone by next Thanksgiving," she added morosely.

Jillian ignored that and said, "I'm thankful Isaac finally got up the nerve to text me, and I'm very thankful he was able to be here today."

Isaac smiled at her and nodded. "I'm thankful Jillian invited me after the Florida fiasco."

"What fiasco? Florida?" Nana asked.

"I'll fill you in later," Jillian said. "Mom?"

"I'm thankful to have all my most favorite people in the world gathered around this table."

Her dad went next. "I'm grateful for my beautiful wife, and that the Eagles are on a hot streak."

Charlie, Ben's dad, laughed beside him. "Same. Fly, Eagles, fly." He lifted his fist to Mack for a bump.

Susie rolled her eyes. "I'm so thankful to have Jenna and George and Taylor and Kyler back home."

Charlie muttered to Mack, "George roots for the Dolphins."

"Pfft. At least it's not the Steelers."

Kate's mom, Cheryl, continued the circle. "I'm thankful our bathroom remodel is finally done."

Susie said, "Did you get one of those walk-in showers?"

Cheryl nodded.

"How is it? Do you love it?"

"It's wonderful."

Roger agreed. "I'd have to say the same. I'm thankful we don't have to try stepping over that high tub anymore."

"That was so nice," Maggie said after her grandfather was done.

"What are you studying?" someone asked Darian. Jillian wasn't sure who spoke.

He looked like a deer in the headlights. "Oh, uh, I'm in nursing."

"You don't want to be a doctor?" Nana asked.

"No, ma'am, I definitely prefer nursing."

Nana muttered, "Who ever heard of a man being a nurse?"

Jillian hoped Darian hadn't heard her. If he had, he didn't show any reaction. Thank goodness.

"Isaac, I hear you own a whole *island*. What's that like?" Ben's dad, Charlie, asked.

Jillian groaned internally.

Isaac wiped his mouth with his napkin and swallowed the food in his mouth. "No, not me. My parents. Well, technically the island belongs to Frazier Industries. It's a small resort, so not like we have a house on a private island or anything."

"You can probably go for vacation any time you want to, though, right?"

"Only in the off-season."

"I'm surprised you're not there for Thanksgiving. It's probably a lot warmer than it is here."

Nana said, "A whole island? That kind of wealth for one person is just obscene."

"Nana!" Summer scolded.

Jillian gaped at her.

Isaac mildly answered, "Believe me, I do not personally

have that kind of wealth. No private islands here, I assure you."

"Why aren't you celebrating Thanksgiving with your own family?"

Jillian wanted to wilt into the chair, but Isaac took it in stride.

"It was mainly logistics. I've been working in New York, and Thanksgiving travel is always fraught. Instead of spending all day dealing with airport crowds and flight delays, I drove a few hours and get to spend time with Jillian." He quickly added, "And you all."

Summer teased, "But mostly Jillian."

He shrugged one shoulder and lifted a hand.

"Are you guys finally dating?" Maggie asked.

Jillian felt her face burn. "I..."

"I like to think so," Isaac said.

"It's about time," Lucas chimed in. "Can we have dessert now?"

Andi rose and said, "I can't wait to try this spiked cider."

"Spiced!" Isaac quickly corrected. "It's not spiked at all, I promise it's not."

Andi burst out laughing. "Freudian slip, I think. I could use a spiked drink after being up since the crack of dawn."

Gavin chuckled as he edged past her to head to the kitchen. "Mom, you just sit and relax. Maybe I'll put a splash of bourbon in your cider." He turned and announced, "We've got a ton of desserts. I'll get everything cut and laid out in the kitchen, then everybody can help themselves."

Jillian watched her dad sneak off to the living room to catch the end of the game.

Isaac leaned back in his chair. "I'm so stuffed."

"Me, too."

Summer crossed behind Jillian's chair. "I hate to ask, but

would you mind grabbing a box of those to go containers from the storage closet in Creekside for the leftovers while I help Gavin get the desserts ready? I can grab them later if you don't want to move."

Jillian put a hand on her belly. "I really don't, but it might help me make room for pie."

Isaac leaned toward her and said, "Where's the bathroom?"

"I'll show you." She led him through the living room and pointed to the stairs. "Upstairs, third door on the left. I'll be right back."

The air had turned colder over the afternoon. It wasn't even five o'clock she needed a flashlight to navigate the dark path. She hustled to Creekside Hall and stood in the storage room considering which of the different sizes of Styrofoam containers would be best to hold leftovers.

All in all, it had been a lovely Thanksgiving.

Except for Nana's weird comments. But again, that was an issue for a different day.

Chapter Twenty-Two

Isaac came back downstairs to Summer urgently herding everyone back to the dining room. "Everyone, everyone, gather quickly. I need your attention. I sent Jillian over to Creekside, so I only have a minute."

He stood back, wondering what was going on.

"We've only got a month to plan a huge, massive, incredible *surprise* birthday bash for Jillian's fortieth. With her birthday being on New Year's Day, she's always gotten the short end of the stick with celebrations, and I want this one to be her best, most awesome birthday ever. I just need volunteers to help me put everything together."

"We're in." Kate was the first to answer for herself and Gavin.

"I'll do cookies," Maggie said excitedly.

Lucas added, "I'll eat them."

"Whatever you need," Andi said.

"Count us in for sure," Ben's mom said.

Kate's mom added, "Us, too."

"Is this even something she wants?" Nana said skeptically. "Or is it so you can throw a party?"

"She definitely wants it," Andi said.

"Okay, great. Does everybody text?" Summer asked.

Everyone nodded except Nana.

"Awesome. Thank you all. I'll make a group text so we can iron out details. Now remember, this is a *surprise*, so this meeting—," she waved a finger in a circle to encompass the gathering, "—never happened."

As everyone scurried back to where they were so Jillian wouldn't come back to find them conspiring, Isaac heard Nana grumble, "Not everybody appreciates surprises." He wasn't sure if he was imagining it, but it seemed like Nana wasn't in favor of this party. Or of him being here for Thanksgiving, for that matter.

He went into the kitchen and made his way through the crush of bodies to where Summer stood, eating a fruit tart over the trash can.

"I just wanted to say, I'm in. One hundred percent. Whatever I can do, whatever you need."

She looked up at him. "Will you be able to come?"

"Absolutely." He wouldn't miss it for the world. "While I have you… Is there something I've done to offend your grandmother?"

Summer's brow furrowed as she shook her head. "I can't imagine. She's been a little touchy lately, but I think it has something to do with her trip to Ohio. Don't give it another thought."

"Okay. Thanks."

She snapped her fingers like she'd just thought of something. "I might put you in charge of charcuterie."

"Shark what?" he joked.

"Funny guy. That place you got the fruit and cheese basket from for Jillian – which was amazing, by the way, and she absolutely loved it – they do individual charcuteries for parties. Might want to contact them asap, though, in case they're already booked for New Year's."

"Sure. How many guests?"

"Probably between thirty and forty."

Jillian came into the kitchen along with a blast of cold air from outside. The glass on the door immediately steamed. "I brought meal containers and the smaller boxes for dessert. I also brought some small soup containers for gravy."

"Fabulous. Thanks bunches," Summer said.

The kitchen was full of people, still chatting and laughing as they filled plates with slices of pie and cake. Isaac didn't think he'd ever seen so much dessert in one place. Maggie had a basket full of individually wrapped custom shortbread cookies she'd made for everyone to take home. For now, there was a chocolate cake, a pumpkin spice cake, some green cake Jillian said was Gavin's special pistachio cake, and pies. Oh, the pies. Pumpkin. Pumpkin with crumb topping. Apple crumb. Two-crust apple. Pecan. Shoofly. Lemon sponge. Lemon meringue. Chocolate pie. Pie, pie, pie.

Jillian chuckled near his side. "If you think this is bad, you should see Christmas. We have all this, plus Maggie and Gavin make a croquembouche."

"I'm afraid to ask."

"It's amazing, really. It's a tower of cream puffs with some kind of spun sugar topping stuff."

"That sounds incredible." He put a tiny sliver of pie on his plate. "I think I've gained ten pounds just standing here looking at these options."

A large hand clapped his shoulder. Mack. "No calories on Thanksgiving. I don't make the rules."

"A Thanksgiving miracle," Isaac answered.

"Just like the Eagles pulling off that blowout," Charlie said from his spot on the opposite side of the island.

"Hear, hear. That was the best Thanksgiving present ever."

"Not for the other team," Jillian teased.

Mack responded with a derisive snort to demonstrate how little he cared for the other team's hurt feelings.

By the time they settled back at the table and ate their dessert, Isaac thought he might explode. He didn't usually overindulge, but there was something about this day that it seemed he couldn't help himself.

Thanksgiving with the Sullivans was so far removed from the Thanksgivings he spent with his own family. Everything had to be pristine and picture-perfect, from the table settings to the freshly pressed clothes everyone was expected to wear. He tried to imagine his mother in the kitchen for hours doing the actual cooking. It wasn't hard to imagine her breezing, or more likely, storming, into the kitchen to berate the staff into executing her perfect vision, but actually pulling something out of the oven? Heavens, no.

He couldn't even imagine the horrified uproar a surprise last-minute guest would cause.

But here, turning someone away was unimaginable. Mismatched chairs and an odd table setting were a small price to pay to make every guest feel welcome, even if it was only five minutes before dinnertime when they arrived. There was nothing calculated about their hospitality.

Not like his own parents' carefully curated guest lists and events designed for show. Not that there was anything wrong with that, but there wasn't any balance. Isaac didn't doubt that his parents loved him, but it was exhausting to try living up to their standards.

"Food coma?" Jillian's voice pulled him from his thoughts.

"Yes. If I move an inch, I'm going to pop."

Mack groaned and slowly pushed back from the table. "Gentlemen, it's our turn."

Isaac looked at Jillian and raised his eyebrows questioningly.

"Ladies do the cooking. Gentlemen do the cleaning. Gavin gets a pass if he wants, because he makes most of the desserts, but he usually helps anyway."

That was more than fair. He gingerly slid his chair back and stood, then collected dirty plates and silverware from the table.

Mack was already in the kitchen, running a sink full of soapy water. He gave instructions like a seasoned drill sergeant, directing someone to empty the clean dishes from the dishwasher and someone else to make a lap around the entire downstairs to collect stray dishes.

A couple of the men were tasked with putting leftover meals together.

Isaac's job was to reload the dishwasher with dirty plates and silverware while Mack washed some of the larger serving dishes.

It wasn't long before the leftovers were divided, the counters were wiped down, and the sink was spotless.

That was the moment, though, that Cheryl shrieked, remembering her turkey in the oven in Creekside Hall.

"Not to worry," Mack assured her. He and Gavin set off on a turkey mission and came back shortly, wheeling the steaming roasting pan on a cart. They plopped it on the island and Mack set to carving the turkey while the rest of the guys distributed it into packets for more leftovers. In all, there was more than enough food for the entire assembled group for the next week.

Isaac hung back, just enjoying the day. He always enjoyed visiting the Sullivans, but this was different. They'd always been warm and welcoming on a business level, but today he felt like they were accepting him into their fold, just as he was. There was no demand for perfection or performance. No expectation of him being anything more than what he was. It was such a good feeling.

"Who do you root for?" Mack asked him.

"I don't know much about sports."

Mack clucked his tongue against his teeth and shook his head.

Ben said, "The correct answer is the Eagles."

"You're darn right it's the Eagles." Charlie held his hand up for Mack to high five. "This is our year."

Gavin stage-whispered, "They say that every year."

"I'll tell you what," Mack said. "Go to a game, and you'll become a fan. There's nothing like the energy of a real live football game. Sixty-eight thousand of your closest friends, all cheering for your team. It's really something to see."

"Do you go to a lot of games?" Isaac asked.

"I try to get to a game every year, but haven't been able to for the past couple years."

"Do you root for anyone else? Like other sports, I mean."

Gavin answered for him. "Only casually. Football's the only one that counts."

Mack chuckled. "You know it."

Jillian interrupted, curling her hand around Isaac's upper arm. "I'm stealing him."

Isaac was enjoying the easy camaraderie with the guys, but he was just as glad to be pulled away. Until they got outside.

"Whoosh, it's freezing out here."

Jillian pulled her sweater around herself and clicked the flashlight on. "I know." White breath puffed out with her words. "I didn't think it was supposed to get this cold today." She hustled toward Creekside Hall.

Isaac opened the door to let her go in first. The handle was freezing cold.

"While I was getting the takeout containers, it occurred to

me that this was the perfect spot for some alone time. Have you been in here?" She pushed a door open that revealed a sort of lounge.

"No, I don't believe so."

"We call it the bridal suite. The mirrors and counters on that wall are for makeup and hair, and of course a nice seating area here so brides can relax before they head out for the ceremony if it's happening here. If not, it's just a spot for the bridal party to hang out and catch their breath if they need it before the reception."

"Very nice." He took in the room. It seemed no detail had been overlooked. There were sturdy hooks to hold dresses, gentle lighting at the seating area, several small tables around the room that he assumed were used to set champagne glasses. There was a long sofa and two matching plush chairs in a calming gray fabric.

Jillian sat on the couch, so he joined her and ran his hand over the cushion. "Are these washable?"

"Yup. Slipcovers. Another brilliant Summer Sullivan detail. The furniture was expensive, but it's durable and easy to clean. You'd be surprised how many spills we get in here. It blows my mind every time a bride in a five-figure white gown tempts fate with a glass of red wine."

"It's very comfortable, too." He leaned back and shifted so he faced her, mirroring her position of one leg tucked under the other, and one arm leaning on the back of the couch while her head rested against her hand.

He gave in to the impulse to reach over and touch the end of her long blonde ponytail that cascaded across her arm.

She smiled at the gesture. "I'm glad you survived dinner. These big gatherings can be a lot."

It was a lot, but in a good way. "No, it was great. I mean it. I always have a good time with your family."

"I know, but you usually get them in much smaller doses."

"I'm really glad you invited me. It's the best Thanksgiving I've ever had."

"Really? How does your family celebrate?"

"Normally everyone goes to my parents' house in Houston. They have lots of parties and events, so there's a huge formal dining room. My mom likes everyone to be 'dressed for dinner' for holidays. The meal is usually catered and served in courses."

"That sounds very fancy."

"It is. Don't get me wrong, I enjoy formal events every now and then, but this was exactly how I always pictured families should celebrate Thanksgiving. Is Christmas like this, too?"

"Times ten. It's all the food and then you add a layer of gifts and chaos with wrapping paper and bows everywhere. Mom has this genius no tags rule for the gifts she buys. She uses a specific wrapping paper for each person, so nobody knows which gifts are theirs until she hands them out. It's always big fun to guess which paper belongs to which person."

"That's very clever." He could imagine Andi having a great time keeping the secret, too. "Most of the gifts under the tree at my parents' are fake."

"What?"

"Yeah, it's more about the aesthetic than anything."

"That's kind of sad."

"It sounds worse than it is. My parents always give great gifts, but it's very important to Mom that everything looks good. Their house is in the society pages every year for their elaborate Christmas displays. One year they came in second on the home tour thing and I thought she'd lose her mind."

"Oh, no."

"Speaking of my family, I'd like to get your opinion on something."

"Sure."

"I'm considering leaving The Frazier Foundation and doing something on my own. Like starting my own consulting firm and maybe scaling back to a small region and growing from there."

"Why?"

It was more difficult than he anticipated to put his thoughts into words. "A bunch of reasons. There are changes coming in the company, so the timing might be good. I'd like to have a home base and travel less. Maybe focus more on long-term partnerships with businesses rather than the way it is now, where I just kind of pop in and then my job is done."

"Did you fill out one of the forms you have your startups do?"

Isaac had to laugh. "That's exactly what Theo said I should do."

"Sounds like you have some homework."

"Is it a crazy idea, though? I've got a lot of security where I'm at."

She looked up at the ceiling, thinking. "It's not crazy, no. And sometimes safety and security can be a kind of cage. You definitely have the kind of background that would make it easier to start out than the average person. Tons of resources at your fingertips, and market expertise." She turned her gaze to him. "Would you make your base in Houston? Or New York?"

He reached over and put his hand on her arm. "I was kind of thinking it might be nice to set up shop somewhere in Pennsylvania. Kind of a whole two birds with one stone thing so I can work on my personal life at the same time."

"Ah. And what personal things do you want to work on?" Her soft smile nearly did him in.

"Well, you see, there's this woman."

"Scandalous. Do tell."

"She's beautiful and smart and sweet and I really like her. But she's based in this little town in Pennsylvania with a successful flower shop, so she can't just up and travel whenever she wants."

"I can see how that would be a concern."

"I thought that if I were to set up a base close to where she is that we would have an easier time of dating and being in a relationship."

"Wow. Is that something she wants?"

His heart squeezed a little. "I sure hope so."

Her brows furrowed inward. "Are you really willing to relocate close to here?"

"I'm seriously considering it."

"Why? You can start your business anywhere, and to be honest, there are probably lots of states that are way more small-business friendly, which you would know."

"Jillian."

"Isaac."

He leaned toward her and put his other hand on her knee.

She sucked in a quick breath. "We don't know each other well enough to be talking about moving and rearranging whole lives, do we? I mean, how do you even know you'll be interested in me a month from now?"

"Four years. I've been interested since the very first time I saw you and dropped all my papers all over the floor because you were so beautiful, and when you smiled at me, you reached straight into my chest and stole my heart. It's been yours ever since. The more time we spend together, the more sure I am."

"When's it going to get old, though? I'm never going to fit in with your family. Ever. So what kind of expectations would you have for that?"

"I would expect you to see them occasionally, sure. But not

often, not for long, and I promise to be a buffer between you and them. I also promise that if we visit them in Houston, we'll get our own place to stay."

"You have it all planned out already?"

"I've been running these scenarios for four years."

"I can't believe you're serious."

"Just say you want us to see where this goes, too. That you want to take a shot at being us."

"I—"

A loud electronic chirp filled the air, followed by static.

"What's that?" Isaac jumped to his feet and looked around.

Jillian got up, much less agitated than he was. "The sound system. It does this every fall. There's something in the speakers that has some kind of feedback when the heater comes on. The electrician says everything's good, so we need to have the sound guy come out, but we haven't yet."

"Isn't a concern during events?"

"Not really. If there's a DJ, we unplug it all anyway just to avoid interference, and if there's no DJ, we have it on, and it never does it when it's on."

Isaac watched her cross the room.

A few minutes later, soft strains of classical music floated through the air.

When she came back in, she said, "Figured I'd give us some background music."

He held out his hand. "Since we have music, may I have this dance?"

She laughed and reached out to take his hand. "You may."

He pulled her close and relished the feel of his arm around her waist and her hand in his. Goosebumps ran across his back as strands of her hair tickled his neck. She rested her head on his shoulder and he was convinced beyond the shadow of a doubt that Willow Creek was destined to be his home.

Correction, that Jillian was to be his home. If she wanted to be in Willow Creek or New York City or Houston or Tokyo or the North Pole, that's where he would go.

Chapter Twenty-Three

Perfection.

There was no other word Jillian could think of that could describe this moment. Isaac's arm was strong around her waist. His hand was warm and soft holding hers as they slowly turned in circles while the music played.

Being in his arms made her reservations and questions fade to the background. Sure, there was a chance Isaac could move to Willow Creek and it could go sideways and be a mistake. But as they moved together and she felt the warmth of his skin against her forehead, she knew a bigger mistake would be not trying.

And as a practical matter, most of the risk was his. He was relocating and shouldering that burden. The only thing Jillian had on the line was her heart.

"I do, by the way," she said.

"You do what?"

She pulled back and looked up at him. "I do want to take a shot at being us."

The relief and warmth and happiness in his smile nearly bowled her over.

She tilted her chin upward and had to remind herself to breathe as he inched his face close to hers.

She made the tiniest of gasps as his lips met hers, and after four years of waiting and hoping, he finally kissed her.

Or maybe she kissed him.

Jillian's toes tingled. Her knees felt like jelly, and her stomach fluttered. Sparks sizzled through her brain. Her fingers tightened on his shoulder and the pressure of his arm seared her back.

If someone asked her name right now, she wouldn't be able to answer.

She let go of his hand and brought her fingers up to brush against his cheek and grazed the beginnings of rough stubble at his jawline.

He wrapped his other arm around her, his palm pressing against the middle of her back, holding her closer.

A while later – a minute? an hour? a week? – they slowly moved apart. She held onto his shoulders to steady herself as the daze of euphoria slowly tapered. A flood of emotions overwhelmed her. She laughed and grinned and her eyes teared up as she kissed him again.

Isaac leaned his head down and rested his forehead against hers. "That settles it," he said. "I'm moving to Willow Creek."

The last week of November passed in a blur and all of a sudden it was Friday, December first. Jillian spent the day putting the finishing touches on the centerpieces for the Anderson wedding scheduled for the next day. It came as no surprise that the bride decided at the last minute that she also wanted an elaborate four-foot long centerpiece for the bridal table and some "minor adjustments" to the bridal bouquet, the throwing bouquet, and the corsages and boutonnieres.

When she wasn't working on the Anderson flowers, she was checking out listings Isaac sent her for short term rentals.

She'd just gotten back from touring an apartment and was adding ribbon to a corsage when Nana came into the shop.

Jillian looked up from her workbench and smiled. "Hey. What are you up to?"

"We need to talk."

"Sure." She wound the thin ribbon around her fingers and slipped another piece of ribbon between her fingers to make a knot at the center of the loop. "What's up?"

Nana sat at the opposite side of the workbench and clasped her hands together.

Jillian pulled the ribbon off her fingers and splayed the loops to make a delicate bow. She held it out to Nana. "Just like you taught me."

"Hmm." She didn't smile back.

"Is this serious? Are you okay?"

"No. I'm not okay. I'm worried."

Jillian set the bow down and focused on Nana. "About what? Or who? Is someone sick?"

"No. I'm worried about you."

She sat back, startled, and nearly lost her balance on her stool. "Me? Why?"

"You're different lately."

"That's not a bad thing."

"Well, I don't like it. You've always been fine just the way you are. You don't need to be more like your sister, and you don't need to date that rich man. He's no better than we are."

Huh? Jillian had no idea where this was coming from. "Nana? What are you talking about?"

"You. All of a sudden it's you and Summer doing this and that. There's nothing wrong with being quiet and reserved like you've always been."

"I don't follow."

"I wasn't sure if I should say anything, but I feel I have to. At Thanksgiving. The two of you were in the kitchen laughing so loud I could hear you all the way in the other room. Summer's always been like that, but I expect more from you."

Jillian blinked rapidly, trying to process. When that failed to give her any clarity, she picked up the corsage and held the bow in place.

"Your sister has always been loud and improper. I don't want to see you turning into someone who behaves like that."

"First of all," Jillian began slowly, "laughing is not a character flaw. It's a good thing. Second of all, Summer is not improper. Third, I am perfectly comfortable with who I am and how I am, and I'm not trying to act like my sister. We're completely different, and I'm just thankful I've learned to embrace that instead of letting it be a source of conflict."

Nana blew out a scoffing breath. "'*Embrace.*' You sound like Agatha. That's all she did when I was out there. Went on and on and on about how I should loosen up and live a little. I live just fine, thank you very much. I don't need to *embrace* acting foolish, and neither do you."

"Nana? Please stop. This is making me very uncomfortable."

"That's because you know I'm right."

A tightness clenched Jillian's chest as her mind connected all the dots. Nana and her sister Agatha were so much like Jillian and Summer. Night and day. Auntie Agatha was loud and gregarious and gave the most incredible bear hugs. Jillian supposed she never drew the parallels because she lived so far away and they only saw her once a year, if that. "No," she heard herself say.

"What?" Nana glared.

"You're not right. Auntie Agatha can be a lot, but she's got a good heart." Jillian thought about when Papa died. Agatha immediately dropped everything to come and stay with Nana for an entire month.

"She has no decorum."

Jillian felt her heart break a little as the pedestal she'd kept Nana on for her entire life crumbled. "Neither do I."

"Oh, stop. You do so. You behave like a proper lady, as you should."

"No, I don't." She pulled in a steadying breath. "When I met Isaac's parents, I jumped into the swimming pool. Hair and makeup done, nice dress and shoes. Dove right in."

Nana gasped. "You did not! Why would you do that?"

"I thought a baby had fallen into the pool," she repeated. "It was just a doll, but it looked real."

"Well, that's a different situation."

"Is it? They don't like me. They think I lack decorum and class."

She scowled. "They're just rich snobs."

No argument there. "My point is that I am who I am. I'm not changing to suit someone else's idea of what's proper. I want to be the kind of person who dives into a pool to save a baby, even if it turns out to be a doll. I want to feel happy and free with my family and laugh in the kitchen. If someone judges me harshly for that, it's their problem, not mine." She tried to be careful with her next words. "I've been judgmental with Summer, and I'm so thankful I recognized it and worked through it before it was too late."

Nana narrowed her eyes and changed the subject. "It

doesn't bode well for that young man sticking around if his parents don't approve. Better to let him go. Besides, he travels all the time. You know what men do when they're off traveling. That's what That Other One did."

"Isaac is nothing like Tate."

"You'll worry every time he's off on one of his 'business' trips."

Jillian made another ribbon for the last corsage.

"That's just how men are. Especially rich ones. They're all alike and you're fooling yourself if you think this one is different."

"I need to get these in the cooler." She got up and took the tray of boutonnieres and corsages to the bank of coolers along the back wall. She put them in more carefully than necessary, buying herself a moment to think of a response.

Nothing came to mind, so she decided the best course of action was to change the subject completely. "The poinsettias the church ordered came this morning. I was starting to worry they wouldn't get here before Advent started."

Nana crossed her arms.

"Mom and Dad are going to help me deliver them to the church this evening."

"Jillian Marie. I'm telling you, that young man—"

"Stop." The word burst out more sharply than she intended. More sharply than she'd ever been with her grandmother. She lowered her tone. "Nana, stop. I love you, and I appreciate that you think you're looking out for me, but Isaac has done nothing to deserve your comments."

"Yet," Nana muttered. She climbed off the stool and shook her head. "Fine, I won't stick my nose in ever again. I'll just keep my mouth shut, so don't come crying to me if I'm even still around when he turns out to be just like That Other One, and don't expect me to take your side anymore when you and your sister butt heads." She jerked her chin upward and walked toward the door. A couple times, she paused and glanced over her shoulder.

Jillian just let her go.

She was done participating in whatever this was.

Chapter Twenty-Four

"Is it crazy? It's crazy, right?"

Isaac turned his laptop to show Alexis the screen with an arial view of the farm situated beside the Sullivans' property, sharing a border of Willow Creek. A farm that just happened to be for sale.

"Yes, it's crazy. And kind of weird. You can't do that without talking to her."

"Then it won't be a surprise," he argued.

Alexis tapped the screen to punctuate her words. "This (tap) should not (tap) be a (tap) surprise (tap). No (tap). Bad idea (tap.) Do not (tap) do this (tap)."

"But—"

"Isaac. No. I'm telling you as your friend, and as a woman. This would be bad. It's a bad idea and you can't do this."

"I don't see how it's so bad."

She sighed heavily.

"She knows I'm looking to move to Willow Creek."

"Then you can bring it up in a conversation. But no, it's not cute to buy the property next to her parents' as a romantic grand gesture. It's weird and kind of creepy."

"Creepy?" He was starting to think maybe this wasn't the brilliant idea he thought it was. "But if we're in a relationship and planning a future, this property would be perfect."

"What if she doesn't like the property? What if she doesn't want to live ten feet away from her parents? Her business is already right there. What if she knows something about the land that you don't? What if she already owns her place and doesn't want to move? Look. I can appreciate where you're coming from. And I think there's room for you to bring it up as a surprise. But absolutely not after the fact. If you want to buy a property that you plan to be part of her future, you need to include her in that plan."

She made a lot of sense.

"If she called and told you she bought you a house, done deal, how happy would you be?"

"Fine. You're right, I'm wrong."

"As usual." She grinned at him.

"I still think it's the perfect solution," he grumbled a bit.

"It's only the perfect solution if she thinks so, too."

She had him there.

"Do you have everything you need for your meeting?" Alexis asked, bringing his attention back to where he sat in his Houston office.

"I think so." Monday morning meetings were never fun, but he had a feeling this one was going to be about as pleasant as drinking bleach. He had a folder with a list of clients that he wasn't actively working with. His active client list was safely stored on his own laptop, which – oops – he hadn't brought to the office.

Theo had worked his IT magic to corrupt several files on the intranet.

"Good luck."

"Alexis?"

"Yes, boss?"

"However this goes, I'll make sure you're not put in a tough position, okay?"

She smiled and opened the door. "I know. You got this."

He hoped she was right about that. He straightened his jacket, grabbed his folder, and put a pen in his shirt pocket. Might as well look like he was approaching it as a legitimate meeting instead of an ambush.

Surprisingly, the only ones in the conference room were his father and Anthony.

He set his folder on the mahogany table and sat in the plush office chair across from his brother-in-law. "How was your Thanksgiving?"

"Let's dispense with the chit chat," his father said as he opened a folder. "At the new year, Anthony will be transitioning into his new position as CFO of The Frazier Foundation."

Isaac managed a smile that felt like it probably looked realistic. "Congratulations."

Anthony nodded once, but didn't meet Isaac's eyes.

"This is part of Phase One for the foundation restructure." He stared directly in Isaac's eyes as he spoke, undoubtedly expecting a reaction.

Isaac kept his gaze steady but didn't say anything.

"By Phase Three, the foundation will be strictly a philanthropic organization focused on fundraising and supporting causes that align with the Frazier Industries mission on a large scale." He paused again for a reaction or comment.

Isaac denied him the satisfaction.

"You'll transition into the role of COO. As a member of the Frazier family, it's important that you reflect a certain image so you can bring in large donors. Because the board insists we have certain fiduciary responsibilities to the clients you're already working with, you'll have six months to get them through the pipeline. As of June first, you'll be based in Houston full-time. You'll spend the remainder of the year cultivating an appropriate image, which will include a home and a suitable partner."

Isaac couldn't help himself. "With any luck, Charmaine's new husband will expire by then."

"Your mother and I have coddled you long enough. You're a Frazier and it's time to act like it." William paused and leaned back in his chair. He said, "Any questions?" like it was a dare.

Fine. If he was supposed to act like a Frazier, why not start now? "I assume my new salary will be effective immediately."

His father raised an eyebrow, clearly not expecting that to have been the response. "Certainly."

"I have to wonder why this wasn't brought up at the strategic session, since it's been in the works for a while."

"It was neither the time nor the place."

"How is the annual planning session not the time or place to discuss major changes to the foundation?" Now that he thought of it more closely, he realized his father didn't even have the authority to make the changes he was demanding, including Isaac's salary.

"The annual session is over. There's no point in hashing over what was or wasn't discussed there. Moving on. Your mother was horribly aggrieved that neither you nor your brother attended Thanksgiving."

Neither, nor. Neither, nor. Isaac felt like he was in English class.

His father continued. "I assume I can tell her you'll both be in attendance for Christmas."

"As of now, I'm planning to be there, but obviously I can't

speak to Theo's schedule." He hoped Theo was going to be there, otherwise it would be a lonely Christmas for him.

"I expect you to encourage your brother to attend. Moving forward, we must present a united front both professionally and personally, and that is why you'll both be relocating to Houston as soon as possible." He jerked his head toward Anthony. "Take a page from his book. Family comes before anything else. Isn't that right, Anthony?"

Isaac looked over to his brother-in-law, who blanched. "Yes," he croaked out.

What the heck was going on? Dad was acting like they were part of some mafia family or something. It was absurd to the point of laughable, but he managed to control his face. Obviously he had something on Anthony. Isaac supposed he should feel some sympathy, but he was too irritated to muster any.

"Is there anything else?" Isaac asked.

"That'll do for now." His father stood and straightened the sleeves of his jacket. "Don't disappoint me, Isaac." He shot a look over at Anthony, then left the room.

Isaac stood and picked up his folder. He stared at Anthony for a long moment, but his brother-in-law wouldn't meet his eyes. His throat moved as he swallowed hard.

"Whatever you've done," Isaac said, "I hope it's worth it."

Anthony looked like he might vomit.

With that, he left the conference room and went back to his office.

Alexis's small office was situated so you had to go through her office to get to Isaac's. He opened the door to her office and she gave him a grimace. "Mr. Tolliver is in your office. I told him I didn't know when you'd be back, but he insisted on waiting. Sorry."

What on earth did the president of the board want with him? "No, that's fine. Would you mind grabbing him a coffee?"

"Already did."

"Would you mind checking with Theo to see if he's available for lunch?"

"Sure."

"Thanks." He turned his attention back to his office door.

Mr. Tolliver stood at the window, looking out over the city. He did not look happy.

"Henry, good to see you." He meant it.

"Isaac. Wish I could say the same."

That stung a little. "What's going on?"

Henry sighed and picked his coffee cup from the windowsill and walked to sit in one of the chairs facing Isaac's desk.

Instead of taking his own chair, Isaac sat in the one beside Henry, scooting it slightly so they could speak face to face.

"I'm disappointed in you."

Isaac sat back, stunned. "That seems to be the order of the day. But why?" He had the utmost respect for Henry, and always assumed that was reciprocal.

"I never thought you'd go along with this ridiculous scheme of your father's. It goes against everything Wilhelmina Frazier stood for." The older man's face puckered in disgust. "I can't go along with it. I *won't*."

"If you're talking about the change in the direction of the foundation, I have nothing to do with it. I just now got out of a meeting with my father and he told me there's a three-phase plan to shift the foundation's purpose."

Henry's steely eyes bored into his. He carefully enunciated his words. "Are you telling me that you had no idea the foundation was going to become a corporate fundraising mill?"

Isaac met his intensity. "Henry, I swear. I've felt like something weird was going on, but when nothing got brought up at the strategy meeting, I thought maybe it wasn't anything to worry about."

"Then maybe you should explain this." Henry reached into his jacket and pulled out a crisp envelope.

Isaac took it and pulled out a sheet of paper. He skimmed down over it. "What is thi—" His question halted when he saw his own name at the bottom. With his own signature scrawled in blue ink. "Henry, what is this?"

Henry didn't answer.

Isaac started over at the top of the letter. It was addressed to the board members, purporting to show support for the changing focus of the foundation, and imploring the board to vote to accept the changes, blah blah blah. "I didn't write this. This did not come from me." He read it again, all the way to the end. "Special session?" He flipped the page over, but the back was blank. "When is this special session?"

Henry regarded him carefully. "I don't believe you've ever lied to me, Isaac, and I hope you're being honest now. Most everyone is planning to go along with the vote because of your say so."

"You're right, Henry. I've never lied to you, and I don't plan to start. I had nothing to do with this. I've read all Grandma Wilhelmina's journals. I'd never agree to something I know she wouldn't approve of."

Henry nodded once. "We all thought it was a little odd you'd call for a special meeting at the marina."

The marina? Isaac couldn't say anything as he watched Henry rise from his seat and head for the door. Not only was the foundation's mission being changed, but his name was being used to facilitate it. And in such a stupid way. Isaac would never call a special meeting at the stupid yacht club.

"Nine o'clock." Henry pulled the door open.

"Thanks, Henry."

Isaac sat, just staring at the wall behind his desk until Alexis came in and put a copy of the letter on his desk. "Um, Mr. Tolliver said you'd be wanting this?"

"Yeah."

"What is it?"

"Evidence," he muttered.

"Theo said he's available for lunch."

Thank goodness. Thirty minutes later, they were seated down the block in a corner booth at a noisy café. Isaac filled Theo in on everything and showed him the letter.

Theo snapped a picture of it. "I'll search the system. It's a longshot, but hopefully whoever sent it was stupid enough to save a copy of it on a company machine."

"I'm just glad Henry was angry enough to come see me in person. If he hadn't, I'd have no idea any of this was going on." He took a long pull of iced tea, wishing it was something stronger. Much stronger. "And now I feel like I need to clean house with my board, too. Why would they go along with this without questioning it? I've never called a special meeting in a letter, and I certainly never called one at the stupid marina."

"Honestly, they probably didn't even think to question it when Dad said you were on board."

He pushed his untouched plate away. "I should get back to the office."

Theo reached over and pushed his plate back in front of him. "Eat. You'll need it. It's going to be a long day."

He wasn't kidding. When he was done for the day, he took the only truly personal items he kept in his office – his signed vintage baseball cards – and put them in his messenger bag, just in case this was the last time he'd see the inside of the building.

He slid his laptop into his bag and adjusted the strap on his shoulder.

Most of the building was dark, and the only people he saw on his way out were members of the cleaning crew. His footsteps echoed eerily in the hallways, and although the elevator never bothered him before, this ride had him on edge until the doors slid open in the lobby.

He nodded to the security guard and swiped his badge to open the door.

It wasn't until he was safely inside his car that he let out a heavy breath.

Sleep eluded him that night.

Tuesday morning was dreary and chilly, a perfect match to his stormy mood. Instead of driving to the office, he went to the marina. Sure enough, the yacht club's parking lot was full of expensive cars Isaac recognized as belonging to his board members.

Isaac's phone buzzed on the passenger seat.

Theo's voice croaked, "It took all night, but I found it. It was on a Frazier Industries machine, not one from the foundation."

"That doesn't make—" Oh, wait. That made perfect sense.

"Anthony sent the letters."

Theo's words confirmed his thought. That also explained why Anthony wouldn't look at him, and why he looked so browbeaten.

"I found drafts of the letter on two devices. Anthony's and…" he sighed. "Our father's."

"I wish I could be surprised."

"Me, too."

He looked at the building looming in front of him. "Thanks. Wish me luck."

"You want me to come?"

"Nah, I can handle it."

"Good luck."

Isaac walked into the yacht club. The hostess recognized him and led him directly to the meeting room. When he walked in, it was the first time in his life he'd ever seen his father truly stunned. He recovered quickly. "Isaac! Son, you don't need to be here for this."

The board members had mostly settled into their seats. Henry sat at the head of the table, nursing a coffee, warily watching everyone.

Isaac's father took his seat and said, "There's no need to prolong this. We all know why we're here. It's a simple yay or nay. Are you in favor of the proposed changes? Diane?"

"Hold on," Isaac interrupted. "This is far too important to rush. There are a few details the board needs to hear before they vote."

He could feel his father's glare burning into the side of his head, but he ignored it and continued. No matter how intimidated he was by his dad – and he was – his responsibility to the foundation was far greater than any personal discomfort. "All of you received a letter that purported to be from me. It was not. Nor did I sanction this meeting."

Someone gasped.

"I did not, and do not, support the proposed changes to the foundation. While we can always make improvements, I am absolutely not in favor of making sweeping changes to our mission and our purpose."

Everyone started talking at once.

While the verbal tornado ripped through the room, Isaac calmly held his father's angry stare.

In the end, the entire proposal was thrown out.

Isaac was almost to the door when a hand gripped his upper arm and yanked him around. "You'll regret this. Don't think for one second we won't disown you *and* your brother, you ingrate."

Isaac yanked his arm back and leaned closer to his father's red face. It was the first time in his life he'd taken advantage of the two inches of height he had. "Don't you *ever* use my name."

Never one to back down, his father spit back, "This isn't over," then spun on his heel and stalked away.

Chapter Twenty-Five

It was Wednesday evening before Jillian heard from Isaac. She'd texted him several times and not heard back.

When her phone buzzed with an incoming call from him, she almost wanted to ignore it, but she answered. "Hi."

"Jilly, I'm sorry, it's been so crazy here. Can you switch to video call? I really need to see your face." He sounded terrible.

"Sure." She tapped her phone until the camera came on.

His tired smile came on the screen. "Thanks. I miss you."

"What's been going on?"

"Too much." He filled her in on the subterfuge and the meeting. "I spent all day yesterday meeting with the legal team to shore up protections to make sure this can't happen again. And today I spent tying up a ton of loose ends with my board."

"You look exhausted."

"I am. I'll be so glad to be done with this."

"It sounds like a mess."

"You look beautiful, though. I miss you."

She felt her cheeks heat at his compliment. "You already said that."

"I miss you enough to say it ten times."

"Any idea when you might be back in the area?" She hoped she didn't sound desperate, but she really wanted to see him.

"Saturday. I'm wrapping everything up by Friday afternoon, and then I'm on a plane. Mrs. Peabody has my room ready for me."

"Nice. Do you know how long you're staying?"

He hesitated. "I don't have a return date for Houston."

She was glad to hear it. "Does that mean I'll have you all to myself for a while?"

"Yes, ma'am."

"I'm excited."

"Me, too." He yawned. "Sorry."

"You should get some sleep."

"I'd rather talk to you." His eyes widened suddenly. "Hey. What can you tell me about that farm next to your parents'?"

The question confused her. "Why do you want to know about that?"

"I'm moving to Willow Creek. Couldn't find a more convenient property than that."

The neighboring farm? That wasn't a viable option at all. "Isaac. It's a working farm. What do you know about running a farm?"

"Nothing. But you said about how great it would be to have fields to grow your own flowers, so I thought that might be a great solution."

"Yeah, I was talking about an acre or two, not a hundred." Having her own flower farm was more of a distant might-be-nice wish anyway. Sure, it would mean more control in some areas, but a lot less in others. And there was always the issue of drought and storms that were beyond anyone's control.

"Oh."

"It's not the *worst* thought in the world, but a farm is a lot.

I'm not sure they'll end up going through with it anyway. Dad said he thought their kids were going to go together and buy it and maybe lease out some of the fields. I know their biggest concern is that it doesn't end up being one of those horrible solar panel farms."

He looked disappointed.

"It's a sweet idea, but I don't think I'm cut out for the kind of manual labor running a farm would require."

"We could hire people to do all the manual labor."

She felt a tinge of annoyance. Apparently she was being too subtle. "Isaac. I don't want to own a farm. I don't want to live on a farm. I want a house with maybe five or ten acres of land, tops. Right now my house sits on three-quarters of an acre, and I barely make the time to manage my own flower beds, let alone growing a whole crop of flowers."

"Oh." He rubbed his face. "Sorry. I went a little overboard. When I saw it was for sale, it seemed like a perfect solution."

"Solution to what? There's no problem here."

"Maybe that was the wrong word. It seemed to check a lot of boxes. Fields for your flowers, check. House, check. Close to your parents, check."

She had to laugh at that. "A little *too* close. I love being here, and there's no way I could have my little shop that I love so much if I was anywhere else. But when I go home at night, I want to look out my window and not see other Sullivans. Believe me, anywhere in a twenty-mile radius is plenty close to my parents."

"Gotcha. So I should widen my search to non-adjacent properties."

"Definitely." She hesitated, not wanting to offend him, but she felt she had to be honest. "Actually... I think you should call off this search."

He sat up abruptly and bumped his phone, because the

screen swung away from his face to show the ceiling to show the floor, then a chair, then finally back to his face. His brows furrowed and he stared intently at the screen. "What do you mean?"

"Maybe stop looking to *buy* a property right now. Get a nice short-term rental and *live* here a while. Get to know Willow Creek. There's no rush."

"I don't want you to doubt how serious I am."

She wished they were in the same room so she could hug him. "I have no doubts about that. I'm just not on board with having no input on a huge decision like that if it affects me. If you want to buy a farm and learn how to run it, I support you. But please don't make some crazy grand gesture on my behalf that would mean I have to change my entire career focus. Because running a flower shop and running a flower farm are two very different things. Isaac. You don't have to buy real estate to convince me you're all in."

He held up one hand, his palm facing the camera, and used his index finger to slash lines across it. "Crossing it all off my list. New plan: extend my reservation with Mrs. Peabody and as soon as I get to town Saturday, find a nice little rental property. How's that?"

"Close. As soon as you get to town, see Jillian. *Then* find a rental."

"Perfect. I miss you like crazy. I can't wait to get… home, Jillian. I can't wait to get home."

Her heart did a little flip-flop.

Chapter Twenty-Six

When they ended their call, Isaac thought he'd fall right to sleep. Instead, all the crazy shenanigans that had taken place over the past few days replayed in his mind. Had it really only been days? It felt like months.

He also didn't relish telling Alexis that she'd been right and he'd been wrong. So very, very wrong. That surprised him quite a bit. It had seemed like a no-brainer to buy the farm next to her parents' property. Start a flower farm. Live happily ever after.

Lesson learned. Grand gestures should be on the scale of charcuterie and maybe a weekend getaway.

Thursday morning he dragged himself into a cold shower, trying to conjure some energy and wakefulness, but it was useless. He trudged through Alexis's office.

"You okay?"

"Exhausted."

"Anything I can do?"

He managed a smile. "You can bask in your superiority."

"I always do, but why this time?" she joked.

"I talked to Jillian about the farm. She has no interest in having a farm."

"Hmm." Her smile looked rather smug.

"From now on, I'll stick with fruit and cheese for my grand gestures."

"You can't go wrong with fruit and cheese."

"I'm learning." He paused in his doorway. "How about you? You okay?"

"It's been a week." She sat and opened her laptop. "But I'm good. Thanks."

He'd barely gotten situated at his desk and started to comb through the financial overview reports he'd asked for when he heard raised voices coming from Alexis's office. He hurried over.

Alexis stood between his door and Anthony. "You can't go in there," she said.

"I need to talk to you," Anthony said to him over her head.

She looked to him for confirmation.

The last person Isaac wanted to spend time with was his slimy brother-in-law. "I have nothing to say to you."

"Please. Two minutes."

Against his better judgment, Isaac said, "Fine."

As soon as he closed the door, he pulled his phone out. "I'm recording this meeting."

Anthony blanched. "What? Why?"

Isaac started the video. "What do you want?" He went around to sit in his chair.

"First, I want to apologize for my part in… this whole mess."

"Which part was that? The identity theft part? Forging my name? Impressive forgery by the way. How many times did you practice signing my name?"

"I didn't want to do any of that."

"Golly, that makes it all better then." Isaac's jaw clenched. He'd like nothing more than to grab the mug full of yesterday's coffee and splash it in Anthony's stupid face.

"Please. Let me explain. Your father told me you were fine with everything, but you didn't have time to send the letters. I thought I was helping you out. And then he offered me a position as the CFO for the foundation. You know I've been working so hard to get a C-suite position ever since I started with Frazier Industries. It's been *fifteen years*. Surely you can understand."

Isaac leaned back and crossed one ankle over the other knee. There's no way Anthony was stupid enough to think he'd been helping Isaac by sending those letters.

"I'm sorry. I thought it was a solid plan. It'd work out to be best for everyone. Your father explained how important it was to keep building and growing the family legacy for generations to come."

Isaac tented his fingers as he regarded Anthony. "Ah, yes, the family legacy. Let me ask you, Anthony, which legacy are you leaving your children? Will you gather them around your knee and proudly pass down your legacy of fraud and theft? Opportunism? Lying? Betrayal? Or perhaps the legacy of being a sniveling cowardly weasel who sold his integrity to his father-in-law for some magic beans? You have so many legacies to choose from."

Anthony lifted his chin. "I... I am not a coward. In fact, you answer to me now that I'm the Frazier Foundation CFO."

Isaac barked a humorless laugh. "You aren't the CFO. You aren't anything in the foundation. Nothing. My father, for all his blustering, has no authority in the foundation. He couldn't even call that meeting, which is why he – and you – stole my identity to do it." He leaned forward. "The promotion he gave you doesn't exist. I hope you still have a job at Frazier Industries, although I kind of doubt it. They're not big on keeping scapegoats on staff."

The color drained from Anthony's face.

Isaac couldn't muster even a drop of sympathy. He pressed the intercom button on his phone. "Alexis, please have security escort Mr. Frazier-Sheffield off the premises."

"Yes, sir."

"What? This is unnecessary. I can leave on my own."

"You could, but I don't trust that you will." Isaac opened his office door just as the uniformed security guard entered Alexis's office.

He watched as Anthony slunk away, accompanied by the security guard.

When they were alone, Alexis said, "Brad's going to be here shortly."

Isaac sighed. He didn't want to meet with their attorney. It was all too unpleasant to deal with, but the sooner everything was taken care of, the better.

By lunchtime, Isaac was starving. Brad's updates should have turned his stomach, and in many ways did, but his body had neither sleep nor sustenance, so it was starting to demand one or the other.

He met Theo at the café and filled him in.

"It sounds like most of it was Anthony doing what Dad told him to do. I have the lawyers shoring up the walls around the foundation so it won't happen again any time soon."

Theo knocked back a huge swig of coffee. "What does this mean for you?"

"I'm not sure. I'm moving to Willow Creek. The sooner, the better."

"Are you okay staying with the foundation?"

Isaac studied his brother. "Are you? Or are you still planning to start something on your own?"

Theo shrugged one shoulder. "I'd feel better sticking around at least until I'm sure everything is in good hands, you know?"

"I do know." He knew very well, because he'd been having the same thoughts himself.

"At least the problems with the foundation are all external. Nobody on the inside was involved as far as I can see from my investigation."

Isaac chuckled. "Fancy word for snooping."

"I do have some concerns."

"Tell me."

"I can't dig too deep on the Frazier Industries tech side. In fact, it's a pretty huge breach that I can get in at all, so that needs to be rectified like, yesterday. But my concern is that I don't know if Four has anything to do with any of this."

Isaac's hand stopped with his fork halfway to his mouth. His knee-jerk reaction was that there was no way their older brother was involved. But he never thought his father and brother-in-law would stoop to identity theft, either.

"I didn't see anything to suggest he's involved. But let's be real, he's a lot smarter than Anthony and a lot less arrogant than Dad, so if he was, I'm not surprised I can't find a trail."

"We need to talk to him."

Theo nodded. "The sooner, the better." He pulled out his phone.

Two hours later, they sat in Isaac's office. Four looked shell-shocked. "I knew there was something going on. Dad told me on Monday that big things were coming, and then on Tuesday he came in looking like he'd been sucking on a lemon."

Isaac gently said, "We're pretty sure Dad's behind this."

Four made a face. "Obviously. Anthony's too stupid to come up with a scheme like that on his own." He shook his head. "Beatrice was right. She said there was something shady going on at the annual event, but I kind of blew it off. I guess I should have paid more attention."

Isaac met Theo's gaze and knew they were on the same page. There was no way Four was involved.

"Now what?" Four asked.

"The foundation's board and legal team are making sure we have better protections in place."

"Dollars to donuts Henry's been in touch with Frank. I'll start reaching out to my people this afternoon." He ran a hand through his salt and pepper hair. "Just what I need on top of all our end-of-year stuff." He stood and walked to the door. When he opened it, he paused and looked back. "Thanks."

"I don't envy his position," Theo said after Four left. "At least we have each other over here, but there's not much we can do to help him on that side."

"Maybe I can help a little bit. I'll talk to Henry and make certain their board is privy to what went down."

Chapter Twenty-Seven

Saturday's temperature hovered just above freezing. The rain wanted to be ice.

Jillian checked her phone every two minutes from the time Isaac's plane landed at noon. She mentally calculated the time to get his rental car and make the hourlong drive from the airport to Willow Creek.

At one forty-five, she decided maybe he'd stopped to eat. By two thirty, she was starting to get worried. By three, she was pacing the floor, trying to call him every few minutes, but her calls kept going straight to voicemail.

At three forty-five, an unfamiliar car pulled into her driveway and a weary Isaac climbed out.

Jillian rushed outside and met him on the porch, throwing her arms around him. "Isaac! What happened? The plane was on time. I've been so worried."

He squeezed her tight. "Huge wreck on 183. To top it off, my phone died and my charger was in my bag in the trunk."

"You look exhausted," she said as she ushered him into the warmth.

"It's been a long week, a long day in traffic, and I'm starving. I didn't stop to get anything because I just wanted to get here and see you."

"I've got plenty of food. There's stuff to make subs, or I can throw a pizza in the oven."

He waved a tired hand. "No preference."

She led him to the kitchen and pulled out all the things she needed to toss some subs together. She made one for each of them, then put a bag of chips and a bowl of pasta salad on the table.

"Thank you. This is the best food I've ever eaten in my whole life."

Jillian laughed. "You must be starving."

"I skipped breakfast, thinking I'd grab something at the airport, but there was a jam at security, so I ended up running for my plane."

"No breakfast at all?"

"No breakfast, no caffeine, no nothing."

"Yikes."

They ate in silence for a few minutes, until Isaac sat up and cocked his head like he was listening for something. "What's that sound?" he whispered.

Jillian listened, but didn't hear anything.

"It's like a really quiet clinking."

"Maybe it started sleeting?" She got up and went over to look out the back door. Sure enough, tiny balls of icy rain reflected in the back porch light.

"That does not look fun to drive in," Isaac groaned from over her shoulder.

"Call Mrs. Peabody and let her know you're okay and not coming. That's nasty out there. No sense in risking it when you're perfectly safe right here."

"Are you sure?"

"You can sleep on the couch."

They cleaned up the table and went to the living room.

"I was planning to decorate my tree this evening. You can help, or if you're too tired, you can watch."

Her heart warmed at his tired smile.

"I would love to help decorate the tree."

Jillian clapped her hands and went to the garage to bring in the large plastic tote that held her tree decorations. In the living room, she popped the lid off and sat cross-legged on the floor beside the bare tree. "First, we need to test the lights."

Isaac plugged the end in and all the colorful lights immediately lit up. "Perfect."

They worked together to wind the twinkling lights around and around the tree.

"It smells so good," Isaac said.

Jillian stood on her tiptoes and stretched to arrange the end of the lights at the top of the seven-foot tree. "I love the soft needles. I remember when I was a kid the trees we got were so sharp and when we were done decorating we all looked like we'd lost a fight with a feral cat."

"Ouch."

"Next we'll put on the ribbon chain." She bent over the box and pulled out a plastic zipper bag that held one of her favorite decorations. "We just have to find the ends first."

"Did you make this?"

"Yeah. I do a lot of Christmas flowers, so I get a ton of themed ribbons. I keep the scraps from the ones I like best and make loops so I can add them to my chain. This particular decoration is six years in the making."

"That's impressive."

They worked together to stretch the chain out until the found the ends, then wound it around the tree in the opposite direction as the lights.

"Are we ready for ornaments?"

"Yes. The ones in the red box go on first."

Isaac plucked the red box out of the tote and took the lid off. "Ooh, they're all different."

"Mom gets us all a new ornament every year. There's one for every Christmas since I was born. Except for the year I was eight." She chuckled and hung one of the ornaments. "And Gavin was ten and Summer was thirteen. They were these handcrafted snow globes and whatever they were made of wasn't stable. All three of them broke. Mom was devastated. The pressure from the loop on top to hang them cracked every one of them."

"Your poor mom."

"She was so upset. She got everyone two ornaments the next year to make up for it."

"I'm not surprised."

They hung more ornaments.

"What about you? What are some of your Christmas traditions?"

Isaac put an ornament high on the tree. "Well, not a lot, actually."

"What about decorating the tree?"

"Mom always hired someone to do all the decorating. Our house was always magazine- ready. Literally. There were always photographers doing photo shoots and writing articles about our house."

"Wow."

"That's the last one in this box. What's next?"

"The small silver box is next."

Isaac got it and grinned as he took the lid off. "I'm not surprised."

The box held handmade felt flower ornaments.

"Each one has a meaning." Jillian took the box from his hand and pulled out the topmost ornament. "These are birth flowers."

"What are birth flowers?"

"Same thing as a birthstone. It's a flower that represents the month you were born in. Mine is a carnation for January. Nana's is a daffodil for March. The rose is June for Maggie. I have one for everyone in the family."

"Did you make these?" He ran his thumb over the name stitched onto the flower.

"Yup."

"They're beautiful." He picked a blue flower with a yellow center off the bottom. "There are a bunch of these. Must be a popular month. But there's no name." He looked up at her questioningly.

Jillian took it from him. "Actually, these are just one of my favorite flowers. Forget-me-nots. I made a ton of them when I was at a particular point in my life that I just felt so alone. Forgotten. So I kind of adopted these as my banner flower."

Isaac picked one up and studied it with a thoughtful frown. "This is the flower in your Jilly's Blooms logo. The little blue flowers inside the Os."

"Very observant."

"It's such a cheerful pretty flower, I'd never connect it to loneliness."

She hung one of the flowers on the tree. "It's the opposite, actually. The forget-me-not symbolizes remembrance. It also represents loyalty and respect. And true love, of course. Legend has it that a man tried to cross a river to his true love, but the current was too strong. He grabbed at a bunch of flowers on the bank but they couldn't keep him from being swept away. As he was carried downstream, he yelled, 'Forget me not!' to his love. She wore the flowers in her hair for the rest of her life, and that's how they got their name. It's also the state flower of Alaska."

"I never knew it was so deep. Now I feel bad about giving flowers without knowing what they mean."

She laughed and put the last flower ornament on the tree. "Petunias symbolize resentment and anger. Orange lilies straight up symbolize hatred. But it's always the intent that matters. They're both stunning flowers and I've had lots of brides request them."

"Do you tell them about the symbolism?"

"Absolutely not." She stood back to look at the tree. "If someone asks, I'll talk about it for days. If someone orders an arrangement for, say, a funeral, I make it with flowers like white lilies that convey sympathy and caring. But if someone wants to send their wife a bouquet of all orange flowers because it's her favorite color, I'll include orange lilies because they're gorgeous, and they can also symbolize passion and joy."

Isaac said, "What goes on the tree next?"

"The last box is regular colored balls. We'll hang them anywhere there's space."

They put the rest of the ornaments on the tree, then stood back to admire their handiwork. Isaac slipped his arm around her waist. "Thank you for including me in this." His voice was thick with emotion.

Jillian turned to look at him. She thought she'd been imposing on him by decorating the tree after his awful week and awful day of traveling. She assumed he'd just been being a good sport. It hadn't occurred to her that he might have needed something like this.

She lifted her chin to kiss him.

Chapter Twenty-Eight

The next two weeks sped by. Before he knew it, it was Christmas Eve. Andi and Mack not-so-subtly expected everyone to join them at church for the evening's candlelight service, which Isaac gladly did. The hymns were soothing and comforting. The soft candlelight filling the packed sanctuary was warm and inviting. Jillian's poinsettias were lush and beautiful. The pastor's voice leading prayer over the group was a balm to the turmoil inside Isaac that stayed with him the whole way back to Jillian's house.

He was glad he'd left Houston. The Frazier Foundation was safe and secure, but Frazier Industries was in major upheaval. Poor Four was thrust to the helm as their father's activities were uncovered. He hadn't done anything illegal that they'd discovered, but he was toeing that line.

His mother was furious that he and Theo were choosing to maintain their distance, at lest until everything was ironed out. She insisted they should be presenting a united front, but there was nothing about this situation that Isaac wanted to be a part of.

Alexis was still in Houston, and surprise, surprise, Theo was also in Houston. Coincidence, surely. Isaac smiled. Jillian had been right. Alexis and Theo were a great match. He hoped it worked out.

"Can I give you your gifts tonight?" he asked as they hurried from the driveway to the front door.

She blushed a little. "I hope none of the gifts are too fragile. I might have jiggled a box or two once or twice."

"I knew you would." He held the door open for her.

Inside, she closed the door and said, "Can I change first?"

He grinned. "Yeah. Let's do that."

It was ridiculous how excited he was that they were about to do the ultimate cheesiest thing in the whole world.

Jillian went to her bedroom and he went to the guest room where he'd been staying since the night he got to Willow Creek.

A few minutes later they met in the hallway and both started laughing like crazy, both of them a little giddy about wearing matching bright red pajamas emblazoned with colorful candy canes and Christmas trees.

"This is so cheesy," she said as she laughed.

Isaac agreed. "There's nothing better than cheesy. Especially Christmas cheesy." In the past two weeks, he'd dragged her to every holiday festival and celebration he could find. He decorated fancy cookies Maggie had made, and helped Gavin and Andi bake and package hundreds of cookies. He even donned a bright red Santa hat with itchy red fur to help deliver the cookies all over town.

After a lifetime of being a prop for Christmas, he was throwing himself wholeheartedly into the entire season.

They sat cross-legged in front of the tree.

"I may have gone a little overboard."

"You think?" Jillian gestured to the mountain of gifts under the tree.

"Technically, most of them are for your family. These are the only ones for you." He slid a stack of gifts toward her.

"Only. My goodness, Isaac."

"I know. I'm sorry. I got so caught up in shopping for presents."

"I see that." She laughed and pushed a stack of gifts over to him.

"Open that one last," he said, tapping a box on top of the stack.

"And you open that one last," Jillian said, touching a tiny square box.

They took turns opening gifts. Isaac was thrilled with his gifts. Jillian had gotten him some books he wanted, a display case for his favorite baseball cards, and a ridiculously cheesy Christmas sweater that would be perfect to wear to the family dinner. A t-rex wearing a Santa suit stood on a mountain of gifts, and when you pressed a button near the hem his eyes lit up bright red and he roared. Isaac laughed so hard tears rolled down his cheeks.

"This... is... amazing..." he wheezed.

Jillian wiped her eyes and they both started laughing again.

"I can't wait to wear this."

When they settled down, Jillian nudged his leg. "Now open that one."

"It's your turn."

"No, open. Please."

He could see she was excited, so he tore the paper to reveal a small box. He opened the box to find a felt flower nestled on tissue paper. The excited humor turned into a deeply senti-mental warmth. "You... you made me an ornament."

Jillian nodded. "It's a yellow rose."

He didn't know much about flower symbolism, but he knew it was the red rose that represented love. For a second, a flash of panic sliced through him. Please don't let this mean friendship.

"Yellow roses can mean lots of things. The most common meaning is friendship, but another traditional meaning for yellow roses is—" She blinked several times and pressed a hand to her throat. "They also mean 'welcome home' and I couldn't think of a more appropriate message than that."

Isaac practically lunged to grab Jillian in a hug. They ended up holding each other tightly on the floor, torn wrapping paper crinkling beneath them and the lights from the tree twinkling above them. It was the single most perfect moment of his entire life.

When he finally composed himself, he sat up and pulled Jillian to sitting. "Your last gift is kind of lame next to this."

"I doubt that." Jillian found the box under the mess of wrapping paper.

"I'm starting to think this was a bad idea."

"Why?" She looked at him quizzically.

He really should have consulted Alexis first.

She tore the paper and opened the box. "It's... a boat?" She held up a plastic toy boat.

Isaac groaned. "Ugh. It was so clever in my head. It's a temporary stand-in. For a trip. Any trip. Anywhere you want to go. We can go see the tulips in Holland or take a Caribbean cruise or backpack through Europe. I didn't want to surprise you with arrangements you might not be excited about. I wanted to—"

Jillian tackled him in a bear hug.

He wrapped his arms around her. "I love you."

"I love you, too."

They talked long into the night, until they both drifted to

sleep on the living room floor, surrounded by wrapping paper and twinkling lights.

Christmas day was the most beautiful kind of chaos.

Isaac couldn't stop grinning as he made three trips from the car with gifts for everyone.

When dinner was over and the dishes were clean, everyone gathered in the living room.

Isaac felt like a little kid. He sat beside Jillian and said, "I'll just be up front and tell you all that I went so overboard. I'm sorry. I hope it's not awkward, but in my family we never really did a big Christmas. Soooooo I shopped like a kid in a candy store who was hopped up on Pixy Stix."

Andi said, "You didn't exchange gifts with your family?"

"I mean, our parents got us kids presents, but our holidays were more for show." He shook his head. "Long story." To break the tension and change the subject, he pushed the button on his sweater. The t-rex roared and everyone laughed.

"That sweater is horrible. Where can I get one?" Ben asked.

Isaac sat back and watched.

Lucas and Maggie, as the youngest, were in charge of handing out the mountain of gifts. When everyone had their pile in front of them, Jillian leaned close to him and laced her fingers with hers. "Get ready. Everyone opens their gifts at the same time and all the wrapping paper gets thrown in the middle of the room. Then we go around and everyone shows their presents."

"Got it."

Mack said, "Ready... Set... GO!"

It was a free for all. Wrapping paper and ribbons and bows

flew everywhere. Boxes were opened and excited chatter filled the room.

Until Mack jumped up and yelled, "NO WAY!" He waved a piece of paper and pointed at Isaac. "Are you serious?! Is this real?!"

Isaac nodded.

"What is it?" Andi asked.

"Tickets to an Eagles game!" He pulled his glasses off the top of his head and put them on his face. "Two seats. This is incredible. We're going to have a blast," he said to Isaac.

Isaac put a hand up. "I was kind of thinking – hoping, actually – that you'd take Charlie. I'm sure he'd appreciate it way more than I could."

"Are you sure?"

"Do I look like the kind of guy who understands football?"

Mack laughed. "We'll get you there, don't worry."

After the gift opening melee, everyone carefully gathered the trash, making sure no gifts or envelopes were caught up in being thrown away.

Mack held a large trash bag that was quickly filled. He tossed it into the hallway to deal with later.

Isaac loved watching everyone share what they'd gotten, even when Nana grudgingly held up the Amish-made lap quilt she obviously loved. He hoped the money he spent didn't make anyone uncomfortable, because he wasn't kidding. He'd gone overboard by a lot, but the truth was that he'd gotten so much joy out of shopping that it didn't matter what he'd ended up buying.

When everyone was done, Andi jumped up and retrieved a basket from under the tree. "Okay, everyone, you know what this is."

Isaac lifted an eyebrow.

Jillian whispered, "Annual ornaments."

He watched the basket pass from person to person and held it for Jillian to pick her ornament out. Instead, she picked two and held one out to him.

It was a tiny laptop with "Isaac" and the year etched on the screen.

"For me?" he asked, surprised. It was all he could do to keep from tearing up.

Best. Day. Ever.

Chapter Twenty-Nine

"Whoa." Isaac stood from his spot on the couch. "You look amazing."

Jillian twirled. Her sparkly black dress shimmered as she turned. "I figured I'd go all out since this is the last day of my thirties." She'd decided to embrace New Year's and let go of the notion that everyone should spend the last day of their holiday break at yet another party. Instead, she'd go spend New Year's Eve with the people she loved and maybe pretend for a little bit that it was for her.

She slipped her heels on and Isaac held her coat for her.

"It's freezing," she breathed as they ran to the car.

It was a short but chilly ride to the farm. The parking lot was full, but there was a spot in front of The Shoppes. Isaac opened her door and held her hand as they crossed the parking lot to Willow Hall.

Jillian smiled as they walked in. Summer had outdone herself with decorations. Soft electric candles flickered on every table. Long tables were set up with food and drinks. At the far end of the hall, a DJ was set up, playing dance music.

She let Isaac take her coat and just stood back to watch. It felt like the whole town was in attendance.

Summer and Ben. Charlie and Susie.

Gavin and Kate. Maggie and Darian. Lucas and a girl Jillian didn't know. Roger and Cheryl.

Her parents and Nana.

Assorted other friends and family.

As she scanned the room, her attention jerked back to a different familiar face near the food table. She grabbed Isaac's arm. "Is that your brother?"

"Sure is." He nudged her and they walked over.

Jillian was delighted to see that it wasn't just Theo. It was Theo and Alexis.

"Oh my gosh, I can't believe you guys came! Happy New Year!" Jillian hugged them both.

The DJ turned the music up and Jillian found herself dancing more than she ever had. Slow songs with Isaac, fast songs with her friends, and a few songs grazing near the food tables.

Before she knew it, the DJ announced that midnight was approaching. He instructed everyone to grab a partner and a glass of champagne to toast the new year.

Isaac handed her a glass and a large screen on the DJ's table began flashing a countdown, starting with sixty seconds. He pulled her to the middle of the crowd on the dance floor.

As the seconds wound down, the DJ shouted to the crowd, "Everybody count it down with me now! Ten! Nine! Eight!"

Jillian shouted along with everyone else.

"Seven! Six! Five!"

"Four! Three! Two!"

"One!"

Everyone spun to Jillian and shouted, "HAPPY BIRTH-

DAY!" as she shouted, "Happy New Year!" It took a beat to realize what she'd heard. "Wait, what?"

There was a quick flurry of activity and people raced, laughing, to flip all the Happy New Year decorations over to reveal Happy Birthday decorations, then ran back onto the floor.

Jillian stood in the center of the dance floor, stunned.

The DJ said, "To Jillian!"

Everyone raised their glasses high and shouted, "To Jillian!" and drank their champagne.

It was a good thing Isaac's arm was around her, because she was pretty sure she might have fallen over otherwise.

"I can't believe you did this," she said to him.

"Not me. I only did the charcuterie things, which are delicious, by the way. This was all Summer."

"Really?" Jillian searched the crowd and found her sister. She went over and grabbed her in a tight hug. "I'm sorry I spent so long being such a jerk. You're the best sister ever. I love you."

"I love you, too." Summer pulled back and lifted her champagne glass. "To forty. It looks like it's starting out pretty darn good."

"It really is."

They clinked glasses and drank their champagne.

The rest of the night passed in a blur of dancing and hugging and presents wrapped in actual birthday paper and great music and amazing food and maybe a little too much champagne. Maybe a lot too much champagne.

It was after four o'clock when Jillian stumbled into bed, giggling and not really worried about wrinkling her dress. She just wanted to sleep.

Isaac pulled her heels off and covered her with the blanket before kissing her cheek. "Happy birthday. I love you."

"I love you so so much," she slurred. "Happy birthday to you, too."

He laughed and turned the light off as he left the room.

Somewhere just before noon, Jillian woke up with the taste of rotten roadkill in her mouth and the delicious scent of coffee in the air. She hurried to brush her teeth and grab a quick shower to wash off the raccoon makeup on her face.

When she got to the kitchen, she found Isaac, looking unfairly refreshed and awake. "We're going to your parents' as soon as you're ready."

"Just need my shoes." She put her sneakers on and followed Isaac to the car. "Are they going to make me clean up after the party?"

He laughed. "I think that's a problem for tomorrow."

"I still can't believe you guys pulled this off. I had no clue."

At her parents' house, there was a buffet of her favorite foods, followed by a sibling photo shoot that was definitely more for their mom, but they had fun recreating childhood pictures and making goofy faces and picking on each other.

When they were done, Gavin brought out a beautiful cake. Everyone sat around the table while Gavin lit the candles.

"Make a wish," Summer said.

Jillian took a deep breath and burst into tears. She had her sister and she was madly in love. What more could a person possibly wish for?

The candles burned halfway down before she composed herself enough to pull in another breath and blow them out.

She looked around at each smiling face surrounding the table. Then she cried again. "I couldn't make a wish," she blubbered. "Because this is it. This is my wish and it's already come true."

Best. Birthday. Ever.

Epilogue

The following November

Marvin piloted the helicopter down onto the pad on Frazier Key.

Isaac squeezed Jillian's hand. "It's going to be a lot different this year."

"I hope so."

Alexis met them at the pad, smiling broadly. "Hey, boss."

"How's everything going?"

"Smooth as silk."

They entered the resort and a loud voice boomed, "Isaac!"

Isaac turned to find Four coming at him with a big smile and a bear hug. "How's it going?"

"Great, great. Can't complain."

"Is everyone already here?"

Four nodded. "I think so. Cocktail hour is already going strong at the pool. Go change into your suits and meet me down there."

"Suits?" Jillian asked.

"Swimsuits. I told you, this year is different. It's a vacation. No formal events, fewer meetings, more fun for everyone."

Jillian joked, "Who needs a swimsuit to get in the pool?"

The cocktail hour ended up being a lot of fun. Everyone was relaxed and having a good time. No one walked on eggshells.

Even the weather cooperated perfectly.

Which was convenient.

Isaac took Jillian's hand. "Let's go down to the beach."

"Oooh, yes. That would be amazing. I love the beach."

"I know."

They'd been to three beaches during the year. Ocean City, Maryland, Majorca, Spain, and Nassau, Bahamas. He'd quickly learned that Jillian loved walking in the sand and that Ocean City was her favorite. It was something she'd learned about herself, as well. She had a whole bucket list of things to do and try. She was determined to make her forties the best years of her life so far.

And so far, she'd been succeeding at every turn. Isaac was so proud, and it thrilled him that he was able to help her cross a lot of those things off her list.

They strolled along the beach, holding hands, pausing every so often to pick up shells.

Isaac let her get a few steps ahead of him, then dropped down to one knee. He pulled the ring box out of his pocket, nearly fumbling it into the sand, but righting it at the last second.

"What's this?" he said.

Jillian turned to look and saw him on his knee. She gasped and pressed her hands to her heart as she hurried back to him. "What are you doing?"

"I would hope it's kind of obvious," he joked.

"Isaac. I didn't—"

He winced. "My knee is on a shell, so if I could do this? Please?"

She mimed zipping her lips.

"Jillian. From the—ouch, sorry." He wriggled to move his leg and a shooting pain raced all the way from his knee to his head. He yelped and fell sideways.

She rushed over. "Are you okay?"

"Oof. Must have gotten it at the exact wrong angle." He struggled to get back in position. "Let me start again." His knee protested.

"Isaac." She bent down. "How about you just ask me."

"Will you marry me?"

"Yes. Now get up before you hurt yourself."

He scrambled to his feet. "If you don't like this, we can return it. Well, not return it, because I had it custom made, but we can get a different ring for sure. I know you don't like big things without any input, but I'm—"

"Isaac!" She put her hands on his arm. "Can I see it?"

He'd been so sure it was the perfect ring, but now he was full of doubt. What if she hated it? Ugh. He should have let her pick her ring. He held the box steady with one hand and pulled the lid open with the other.

Jillian gasped and covered her mouth.

"Was that bad? It's bad. It's okay, I promise, we'll get one you like."

Tears shimmered in her eyes.

"I…"

"It's perfect," she whispered.

Isaac had spent months going back and forth with the jeweler to get the drawings perfect. Five aquamarine petals, surrounding a ring of tiny yellow citrine stones, with a diamond solitaire center, all set in a platinum band. He swallowed hard. "Is it right?"

"Yes, it's a perfect forget-me-not. I love it." She held out her hand.

A relieved breath whooshed out. He'd been so afraid it wouldn't look like her favorite flower. His hands trembled as he pulled the ring out of the box and prayed he wouldn't drop it in the sand. By some miracle, he slid it onto her finger without incident.

He held her hand and looked in her eyes. He said, "The forget-me-not symbolizes true love, respect, faithfulness, and the promise of remembrance. Those are things I will bring to our marriage. I love you so much, and I can't wait to be your husband."

"I love you." Jillian held up her hand, turning it this way and that. "And I love this. It's perfect."

Her face glowed in the sunset's brilliant light. "You're perfect. And for the record, I not only got your parents' blessing. I also got Nana's."

Jillian kissed him again. "I knew she'd come around."

The next four days were full of fun activities and a handful of meetings. Four gave reports that Frazier Industries was in great shape following William Frazier's "early retirement."

Isaac and Jillian spent some quality time with Theo and Alexis, Four and Beatrice, and their daughter Evangeline and her fiancé, Thomas.

Through Four, Isaac learned that Anthony had discovered his backbone and separated from Caroline. She quickly realized that she did actually love him, and they were hopeful counseling would help them move forward, together.

Their parents had essentially gone into hiding, trying to salvage what they could of their tarnished reputations. Isaac wished them will, and hoped that in time they'd be able to repair their relationship. For now, he was comfortable keeping his distance.

Charmaine's fourth husband, Alan Henderson, did unfortunately pass away. Charmaine's mourning was for the fact that his estate was locked down solid, and all she got to keep were the gifts he'd given her.

At dinner their last evening, Theo shocked everyone by dropping to one knee and proposing to Alexis. Of course she said yes. Isaac was thrilled to have her as a sister-in-law, but he really hoped she still planned to be his assistant.

Jillian leaned over to him. "I just had an impulsive thought."

"What?"

"I think we should invite them all to Thanksgiving."

Isaac kissed her forehead. "I just had an impulsive thought of my own."

"What?"

"I think we should get married on Thanksgiving."

"Wow, short engagement."

But that's exactly what they did.

Also by Carrie Jacobs

HICKORY HOLLOW (Can be read in any order):

Drunk on a Plane

Caller Number Nine

The Boy Next Door

Luck of the Draw

Cat Burglar

Mending Fences

Two Tickets to Paradise

Bad Advice

Where There's a Will (novella)

STAND ALONE:

The Bucket List

WILLOW CREEK:

#1 Everything's Under Control

#2 Recipe for Disaster

#3 Forget Me Not

For details about all of my books, visit my website. For exclusive sneak peeks, behind-the-scenes information, and much more, sign up for my newsletter at carriejacobs.com.

Author's Note

Dear Reader,

I hope you enjoyed Jillian and Isaac's story as much as I enjoyed writing it!

From the first time Jillian and Isaac interacted back in Summer's book, I had a Jane & Bingley vibe in mind from them. I loved finally bringing them together, despite their different backgrounds and challenging families!

To keep up with all the latest updates and news, be sure to sign up for my newsletter at carriejacobs.com! You'll get exclusive sneak peeks, behind-the-scenes info, notice of upcoming releases, and all that jazz. You can also follow me on Facebook facebook.com/carriejacobsauthor for updates, notice of my upcoming events and more importantly, pictures of my furry editorial assistants.

If you enjoyed Forget Me Not and have a moment to spare, leaving a review online would be very helpful to me. (Even if you didn't buy it online, you can still leave a review.)

Best,
Carrie

About the Author

Carrie's love of storytelling began in early childhood and never wavered as time marched onward. She reads in pretty much every genre imaginable, but found her writing happy place in small town contemporary romance and romantic comedy.

From that love came Hickory Hollow and the town next door, Willow Creek. Both towns are a mashup of her hometown and places she's either visited or would like to. Her favorite part of her fictitious locations? The residents don't have to drive an hour to get to Target, like she does in real life.

Carrie lives in beautiful central Pennsylvania with her very own romcom hero and thoroughly spoiled furry editorial assistants.

Connect with Carrie through her newsletter or social media!

Website: <u>carriejacobs.com</u>

facebook.com/carriejacobsauthor
instagram.com/carriejacobsauthor
goodreads.com/carriejacobs